STRANGE HEAVEN

STRANGE HEAVEN

LYNN COADY

GOOSE LANE

Published by Goose Lane Editions with the assistance of the Canada Council, the Department of Canadian Heritage, and the New Brunswick Department of Municipalities, Culture and Housing, 1998

The author acknowledges with gratitude the support of the Canada Council.

Edited by Laurel Boone.
Cover photograph © Cora Cluett, 1995. Reprinted with permission of the artist.
Cover and interior design by Julie Scriver.
Printed in Canada by Imprimerie Transcontinental.
10 9 8 7 6 5 4 3 2

Canadian Cataloguing in Publication Data

Coady, Lynn, 1970-
    Strange Heaven
    ISBN 0-86492-230-2

1. Title.

PS8555.023S87 1998   C813' .54   C98-950071-3
PR9199.3.C548S87 1998

Goose Lane Editions
469 King Street
Fredericton, New Brunswick
CANADA E3B 1E5

THIS BOOK IS FOR CHARLES

For that faire blessed Mother-maid,
Whose flesh redeem'd us; That she-Cherubin,
Which unlock'd Paradise, and made
One claime for innocence, and disseiz'd sinne,
Whose wombe was a strange heav'n for there
God cloath'd himselfe, and grew,
Our zealous thankes wee poure. As her deeds were
Our helpes, so are her prayers; nor can she sue
In vaine, who hath such title unto you.

— JOHN DONNE

CHAPTER 1

It seemed as if things were happening without much reason or point. There were no warning bells going off anywhere to announce: This is going to happen. And once things did happen, there was no discernible aftermath. Her mother often phoned with lists of people who had died, or else had contracted an infestation of some kind and for whom death was imminent. Most of them were old, some related. Bridget's mother went with the ladies to say rosaries for every soul.

"It's a shame, you know," she would say to Bridget, "the way everybody is dying."

At the end of a not particularly hot or bright summer, Archie Shearer killed Jennifer MacDonnell. Bridget's mother called her up and told her that. Bridget herself was now at the end of a sick, uncomfortable time and had no trouble imagining it. Everyone was saying it was terrible. School was just starting, the school from which both of them might have graduated, and so vans and cars from the CBC and other local stations were parked out front for the first couple of days, distracting everybody. Bridget supposed that if you managed to position yourself just so in the main hall or out front, you might have seen yourself on the news that evening. Or heard yourself on the radio saying that it was just terrible.

They talked about it for a minute, Bridget getting her mother to recount details already given, for she was too used to her mother's

obituaries and hadn't been paying attention at first. But after she had
expelled her feelings of surprise and her mother had remarked on
how terrible it was, they moved on to other things such as Bridget's
bowel movements and what had she heard from the social workers.
And by the time Bridget hung up, she recognized that she had forgotten all about Archie Shearer and Jennifer MacDonnell during the
last part of the conversation even though they were her neighbours
and close to her in age. It was still like a thing on a screen. Now that
it happened and she knew of it, it didn't concern her any more. That
was what other people's dying meant.

She stopped at the nurses' station on the way back to her room
and said to Gabby — a nurse, supposedly, although she didn't look
like one, she was all beads and bangles with a ring through her great
nose — "I think this medication is doing something to me."

Gabby's eyebrows were, or maybe just looked, painted on. She
raised them. "Still constipated, my ducky?"

"Yes, but I mean I think it's doing something to my mind."

For such a whimsically dressed woman who sometimes danced
down the corridor on her way to ask everybody whether or not
they'd had a bowel movement that day, Gabby could project quite
an air of sternness when she wanted to. "No, Bridget," she said.
"The medication doesn't do anything like that."

Then what are you giving it to me for, Bridget thought, heading
down the corridor and listening to the bones in her bare feet crack
across the tile.

She asked to watch the news on the plastic-encased television in the
common room and saw that Heidi had managed to get herself before the cameras. Heidi had sent Bridget a big get well card and got
everyone in their graduating class to sign it. Bridget had felt sick,
reading all the names, thinking of herself in every head, of people
passing their time in discussion of her.

"Did you know the two people involved?"

"Oh, yah, everyone knew 'em. I just think it's terrible, though. People shouldn't get shot."

That was all of Heidi. Then photographs of the two of them, a prom picture of them together, which was pretty good, emphasizing the irony of the fact that he had killed her. Then a picture of the donut shop and the empty field behind it — gone yellow from a sudden early frost — that he had chased her across.

Bridget was thinking she might have been there that day — if not for being here — it would have been easy for her to have been there with Heidi or with Chantal or with Mark and his friends, or just by herself. Probably everybody was thinking that. One person who was there, she later learned, was Jason MacPherson, who hung out there all the time and had irritated everybody by saying he hadn't been paying attention, although with him it was no surprise.

Everybody was talking about it, her mother had said. And there was a piece on the local news about violence in our schools, even though it happened outside of a donut shop. And a national news magazine included the incident and the prom picture in a story called "Killer Kids" and tried to understand it. Which Bridget's father would find foolish because, he said, kids were killing each other back and forth up there in Toronto all the time, and there was no need to come down here and set us up to look like a bunch of backwoods freaks just like the Golers down there in Newfieland. Nobody within hearing distance ever corrected him about where the Golers were from.

What was happening to the young people? This, according to the news, was what people of the area were asking themselves. It was because of television, and music, and videos. It was getting as bad as the city. This is what people said. Parents fretted. Albert, Bridget's uncle, who was now living in the city himself, came to visit Bridget a few days after she had heard about it, and said, "Horseshit. I remember when I was living up in Tatamagouche working at one of the sawmills up in the friggin hills there, all of sixteen years old, and Baxter Forsythe comes back from the war, what does he do? He knocks the goddamn bandstand down, that's what he does. No place for Kisslepaugh's brass friggin band to play, which is fine, because they was no damn good anyway. Oh, they say, so big deal, he knocked the bandstand down. You mark my words, I said, mark my words. That fella's gone queer over there. Back then queer didn't mean homosexual. Well, it did, but it also meant other things. Queer in the head. That's what he was, and there I am, sixteen years old, the only one with any sense in that town. I'm the only one who knows it. Oh, get out, they say. You mark my words, I tell them, that fella's a bomb waiting to go off. Oh, no, they say. Well to Hell with yas, I'm going back to the Island, that's what I told them. And Frank Jollimore was sad, you know, because he needed me at the mill. Well Frank, I says, I'm sorry, but I can't live in a town full of damn twits who don't know when the Armageddon is on its way. So there I am back down at the Forks where I belong all snug as a pig in the old s-h-i-t working for John Campbell. I think it was John. He lost one of his arms. Anyway, there I am and doesn't a letter arrive from old Frank Jollimore. By God, Albert, you were right. Last night old Forsythe burned the town to the ground. The whole goddamn town, gone, poof."

"The whole town?"

"Well, the main friggin street anyway. Gone, poof. Burnt down by a crazy man. And then he shot himself. So there you go, it doesn't just happen in the city, that there kind of thing. Happens all the time, everywhere you go. I've seen a lot, you know. I'm just like that song, 'I've Been Everywhere, Man.'"

It was true. Albert would come to visit her regularly and talk all about his travels. He had worked in mills all across the Maritimes and then moved on through Ontario, completely eschewing Quebec. "Held my nose the whole goddamn way, going through on the train," he said. He had even spent some time out West. For all his travels, he seemed to have enjoyed practically none of it. Ontario constituted "a pack of a-holes," and westerners were a "pack of g.d. shit-kicking yahoos." Only in Newfoundland was there to be found "any fucking civility," although he had never gone out there to work, only to visit Newfoundland friends who he'd made working in the mills, and who, he said, could never stick it out for very long and always ended up fleeing the mainland in fear and consternation.

Only recently had she begun to notice that when Albert spoke to the likes of Bridget or her mother, his language was a pastiche of curses modified into their less offensive versions alongside other curses that he either forgot to modify or considered too common-place to bother with. Every now and then he'd forget himself in his excitement and come to their house after a hunting trip in the Margarees exclaiming that he had shot a bird or a deer to fuck and back, and then he would look around quickly and blush and hurry to the bathroom.

Gabby said that the priest was to come the next day. Not the priest from home, but a hospital priest who paid kind visits to sick Catho-lics. Bridget's mother had found him as she wandered the corridors looking for sick babies to hold and asked him to go see her. Bridget said something about it to another girl on the ward, Mona, who said she thought Catholics were like Druids and nobody really was one any more. Mona was from suburban Toronto. Bridget, at first, didn't understand what she was doing way out here.

"Don't they drink blood?"

"They drink wine and pretend it's blood."

"Well, that's just crazy, isn't it? Have you ever gotten into Wicca?"

Bridget tried to tell her about this highly civilized priest they had once had. He would put on plays in the hall and had laughed out loud at her solemn first communion when she appeared before him in a white dress and her mother's bridal veil with chickenpox scabs all over her face. She and her friends played on the discarded chunks of concrete in the woods beside his house and took it into their heads to pay him a visit to find out about God. Bridget was very interested in God at that age because religion seemed to embody the only stories of magic and complete improbability that everyone ac-tually believed in — children and adults alike.

Instead, the priest would take them inside and put on classical music and encourage them to close their eyes and try to imagine what was going on in the composer's mind. And his housekeeper would bring them squares.

The problem was that this priest had been from the mainland, and once at a high school basketball game — he was the coach — somebody had spotted him with a flask. He also taught choir and could sing very well, and would always scurry around the altar trying to get everyone to sing. And most people thought his sermons were too long, but they also didn't like it that on hot days or storm days he would quickly go through the motions of mass and then let them go early. Soon he was replaced by a Father Boyle, red-faced and tired-seeming, and everyone was content.

But it was not easy to get Mona to sit still and listen to Bridget explain about priests. Mona was likely to start doing sit-ups in the middle of it until she heard something that she could relate to her own life. Bridget knew all about Mona, who had problems with her father. Her parents were divorced, and Mona had mostly lived with her father, whom she hated. Mona described her father as a faceless monolith. It took Bridget the longest time to figure out that Mona was incredibly rich. Before this revelation, she had not been able to fathom what it was about Mona that she found so completely alien. At sixteen, in the middle of the school year, Mona had jumped into her white jeep and driven to Florida all by herself, without telling anybody. She stayed there for five months, making friends and doing coke. She said she met all these men who were being put up in a hotel by the FBI, and everything was free and they said she could stay with them. The rest of the tale was lurid, and Mona was embarrassed telling it to Bridget, at one point yanking a pillow out of its white case and pulling the pillowcase over her head so she could continue with the story. It ended with Mona getting the living shit beaten out of her by these hotel men because she had taken all their cocaine. The police found out about it and sent her home, and her father sent her here. And there sat Bridget talking about priests.

What Bridget appreciated the most was that Mona had absolutely no interest in hearing anything about Bridget's life up until now. She never asked Bridget what she was doing here or what she had done. Mona only wanted someone to talk to and be friends with.

They let her and the priest, a none-too-thinner version of Father Boyle, go into the kitchen and talk because the kitchen was usually locked when it wasn't meal time. Everyone knew this, so no one would disturb them by walking in.

When the priest saw that she had nothing to say, he began telling a story about working as a missionary in the Philippines. He said there was this beautiful little girl there and everybody in the village loved her, but she had leukemia and was going to die. Everybody knew it and did everything they could to make her happy and to keep it from her. And the priest said that every day the little girl used to walk out to a cliff and stand looking out on the ocean for a while, and then she'd come back to the village. The priest said this struck him as very sad, so one day he followed her out to the cliff and he said to her, "Well, you know, dear, everything is going to be all right, now." And the priest said she just looked at him and smiled. "She knew better," the priest said, finishing. "She knew better."

The priest sat with his fingers entwined and actually twiddled his thumbs for a few moments, smiling. "Ah dear, dear, dear, dear, dear," he said, looking around.

Once Bridget thought she would be a priest herself. She had decided one day when she was eight, and the priest, the one she loved, came to the school, and all the Catholic kids were told to assemble in the gym. And no matter how hard she thought about it, Bridget could never figure out what the reason for this assembly had been. It had not been near Christmas or Easter time or anything. But in any case, they all sat on the floor and the priest began to ask them questions. And Bridget, who was sitting directly in front of him, answered them all. She had been the only one who knew all the answers, and she could remember thinking to herself that she didn't even know where she had learned all this stuff. And on her fifth or so answer, the priest, who had laughed at her chickenpox, raised his arms and laughed again and said, "Maybe Bridget should be up here giving the lesson!"

That was it. That had to have been The Calling that everyone spoke about. Bridget was going to be a priest. She went back to her classroom and told the teacher that she wanted to be a prime minister when she grew up, because for some reason she had the idea that prime minister was the proper name for a priest. The teacher seemed very impressed, as Bridget had expected, and said why didn't Bridget go and sit down and draw a nice picture of herself as a prime minister. So Bridget created herself as an adult in white robes (which she used chalk to colour), her arms raised in front of a sea of pink circles which served as faces. On a whim, she made her hair fantastically long, and it took up most of the picture. Last, she drew a large cross on her chest.

"Oh, that looks like a priest," her teacher said.

"That's what it is."

"A priest isn't the same as prime minister, dear. Don't you want to be prime minister?"

"I thought it was the same," Bridget said. And the teacher had been good enough not to say very much else about it and put the picture up on the window so that the sunlight could shine through its colours like the stained glass at church.

Every now and again, thoughts would occur to her that, if she considered them, were disturbing. She hadn't started considering them until the phone call about the killing back home, which had meant nothing to her. She had thought it might be the medication, but Gabby had said no. Now she was noticing other things. Things she thought, or sometimes things she didn't think. She used to like music. She used to listen to music a lot. And somebody brought her a ghetto blaster and a bunch of tapes — new tapes that she had actually asked for because she thought she wanted them. But she never listened to them. She let Mona, or whoever else wanted to, listen to them. It never occurred to her to listen to them.

She was not bothered by where she was. It seemed fine. She looked out across the city from where she was sitting, and it was beautiful because it was October. It would be beautiful back home, too. The high school kids would be drinking down at the trails because the weather was still warm. Mark had caught pneumonia once from drinking at the trails. As he struggled back up the hill in the dark through the woods, he tripped over one of the little bridges and fell into the brook, his friends laughing their holes out. That had been in late November, last November. He got quite sick.

What is happening to my mind? she thought. But she wasn't worried about it. She was curious. She used to get angry all the time, she would get angry like a man and sulk, not say anything about it, just go off by herself. But one time she screamed "Fuck!" at her grandmother, who was ninety-eight, an invalid. It was a terrible thing to do, but as usual no one else had been around, and her grandmother, Margaret P. they called her, had been screaming at Bridget that she was the devil, and that she stank, that she was a bitch-devil, which Bridget could not believe. But she couldn't imagine doing that now. She was mildly worried about her family, who had to pay a homemaker to look after Margaret P. and Rollie now that Bridget was up here.

Dr. Solomon had said, "You're almost eighteen. You won't have to stay here if you don't want to."

"Oh, good."

"You can do whatever you like. The world is your oyster."

Bridget had never heard this expression before. She went back to her room to puzzle it out.

Her uncle hadn't liked the doctor, he in his workboots and she in her heels. He wore work boots as a matter of course, having been a woodsman all his life. It was his footwear of choice. She had shaken his hand and said she was pleased to meet him and clicked off down the corridor in her short-heeled leather pumps. Albert had a tooth-pick between his teeth and removed it, watching her go.

"Twat. Solomon? Jew. Ask her when she's gonna send you home where you goddamn well belong." Albert was always talking about where people goddamn well belonged.

Bridget didn't say that she was getting the feeling she could go any time she liked. The world was, after all, her oyster.

Albert began to giggle. "Ask her if she's ever gone swimmin with bowed-legged wimmen and dived between their legs." Albert was always instructing people to ask this of anyone he felt was uppity. "Ask her if she knows how to play the swinette." He began to rock with raspy, voiceless laughter. "Do you know what's a swinette?"

"Yes."

"You string a violin string across a sow's arsehole!"

Bridget was never to know if these were things he had heard somewhere, perhaps during his travels, or had made up. He had been a terrible influence on her as a child. She got in trouble at school when she was six. The nun who was teaching them had asked if anybody in the class knew any rhymes, and Bridget got up and began to recite:

> There was a little bird
> No bigger than a turd
> Sittin on a hydro pole.

This was one of Albert's favourite stories to tell people.

> He stretched his little neck
> And he shit about a peck
> And he puckered up his little
> Arse-hole.

Bridget had stayed in the city with Albert and his wife for the sum-mer, waiting for the time. It was a cliché, leaving home to stay with relatives for a while, but at that point, who cared? They were very good to her. Bridget had been bothered about what Albert might say, but surprisingly, he doted. He brought her ice cream and chips and let her have a beer every now and again, brought it home especially for her, because he had been on the wagon for something like thirty years. And her aunt Bernadette was always throwing afghans on top of her. Sometimes Bridget and Albert would be sitting together drinking tea in front of *The Young and the Restless* and he would slap her on the knee and say, "Don't you worry, one of these days we'll find that little bastard and knock him to shit." It was funny. She was good and he was bad, they were assuming that. They were assuming that he'd ridden off into the sunset at the first sign of trouble. But there he was back home, working at Home Hardware. Full time, now that he had graduated. They seemed to think she should have been full of rage, wanting to get back at him, but all she had really wanted was to get away from him and was content now that this was so.

Her aunt and cousins took her to see Mother Theresa when the ancient saint came to visit in July. The people there waved homemade signs and glanced at Bridget's gut approvingly. All in white, Mother Theresa stretched her tiny hands out to everyone and said, "If people do not want the little babies, I tell them, give them all to me! I will take all the little babies."

Bridget could remember, after finding out it was impossible to become a priest, deciding that she would be a saint when she grew up.

CHAPTER 2

Visitors were the worst thing.

Heidi often came up on the weekends with her mother to shop. She told Bridget that she could join them any time she wanted, but Bridget told her it wasn't allowed — the whole time knowing she could get a pass from Solomon whenever she wanted. She was low-maintenance, as far as patients went, and that was probably why they were impatient for her to be on her way. She did nothing. She exhibited no signs. She did not cry all the time like Kelly the anorexic, or explode like Byron and have to be put in the quiet room where he'd sit cross-legged and howl like a hound. She had begun to think maybe she should do something but couldn't think what. Her only misdemeanour had been sarcasm, which Gabby didn't appreciate. "I don't appreciate that, Miss Murphy. And if you think I appreciate that, you're wrong."

But even sarcasm had petered out because one day Bridget called Gabby Nurse Ratched, for a joke, in front of everybody, and Gabby and everyone else thought that she had said Nurse Ratshit. So although Bridget was briefly a hero to everyone on the ward, Gabby's feelings were hurt, and the next couple of days were a misery — Gabby being the kind of person who could project her feelings almost tangibly into the people around her. So Bridget stopped trying to make jokes.

And once Babs the social worker had come with some final

papers to sign and some pictures, which Bridget supposed she was obliged to look at.

"Would you like them, Bridget? The parents say you can have them." And Bridget supposed she was obliged to want them.

"So what are your plans?"

"Oh, Christ," she said suddenly. The cusp of adulthood. Everybody was expecting so much.

Babs appraised her with her blinky hamster's eyes. "What's the matter?"

"I have no plans."

"Well, that's okay," she said comfortingly.

"I don't want to have any."

"Oh. Well, that's okay, too, for now. You've just come through a rough time, haven't you."

But the only rough thing about it had been her body's betrayal. She'd thought for a while it would drive her round the bend. She would attempt to eat hamburgers and fried chicken, and as soon as the food came under her nose, she would have to put it down again. The smell was toxic. She would be drinking at Dan Sutherland's place — or she was supposed to be drinking. She would have one vodka and orange juice and be physically unable to take any more. It was not that she felt sick, she just couldn't do it. Couldn't lift the glass, couldn't swallow. The guys would be appalled and wouldn't know whether to make fun of her or what. At school, she would stagger to the office between classes and ask to lie down in the sick room, where she had so often rested on the first days of her periods. And she would fall immediately asleep, dream insanely, and wake up three hours later, the secretary having forgotten about her in there. All this happened early on, before she had admitted anything to herself.

Later was much worse, however, not because she felt sick but because she felt wonderful, like she could lift a car, like she could face any torment. Everything was going to be fine, her endorphin-saturated brain kept telling her. Everything was going to be great! All lies her body was perpetuating in order to keep her from walking off the top of a building. It was like a science fiction or horror movie, being controlled and not knowing it, not until it was too late. Like *Rosemary's Baby*. And she did not blame it, she did not blame him. It was nature's fault. Nature being known in some circles as God.

Her brother would visit. He was going to school not too far away, and she supposed her mother kept calling to remind him. What she remembered about her brother was that one time he was sitting on her stomach and batting her head back and forth between his hands, and she was trying to think of something to say to make him stop, and finally she yelled, "Yeah, well at least I say my prayers at night."

And it worked, he stopped batting and looked down at her with his perpetually offended and slightly repulsed expression and said, "I say my prayers at night. I bet I say them more than you do. I say them every friggin night. And God likes me better than he likes you because I always win the Award of Excellence in track and field." And then he climbed off her and made as if he was going to kick her in the kidneys just to see her cringe.

She knew it was bothersome for him, and she wanted to tell him that he didn't have to come. Gerard could not stand sickness. Aberration of any kind was something he avoided. He had been glad to leave home with its noisy fights and Gramma hollering mysteries from her room and Uncle Rollie snorting and making mute circles in the living room with his hands over his ears. She often got the feeling that her brother found her, along with all the rest of them, grotesque in some respect. She would use a knife to spread Cheez Whiz on her toast, and although he was having the exact same thing, he would take a clean knife out of the drawer to spread his. Later on, when they were older, he would stand in the bathroom door and watch her put makeup on.

"That's too much."

"Fuck off."

Gerard would close his eyes. "Guys don't like girls who curse."

"I hope they at least like girls with big boobs."

"I can't wait to get out of here," he would say. "I am going to find a sweet girl."

"A sweet girl."

"A virgin."

"Ha!"

Gerard looked at her. He cleared his throat. "I hope you're aware," he said, "of how important it is for a girl to remain a virgin, at least until she's ready to get married."

As a teenager, Bridget was having the time of her life where Gerard was concerned. When they were children, he had always been able to get the better of her, but nothing she could say or do seemed ever to have any effect on Gerard. Now her every movement caused him pain. She began to laugh at him.

"I hope you're aware," she mimicked, "that you may kiss me little brown bung-hole." This a preferred rejoinder of Albert and her father. Gerard shuddered again and went to his room to listen to Bob Seger albums. And Bridget went off to Daniel Sutherland's, whose parents never seemed to be at home.

Margaret P. could not remember where Bridget was, Gerard said. He had heard this from their mother. Sometimes Margaret P. didn't even remember Bridget was gone and would call from her room, "Have Bridey C. bring me a toddy!" But mostly Margaret P. knew that Bridget wasn't there. She just couldn't remember where she was. It didn't help that when the relatives came to visit they would tell her things about their own families, people Margaret P. couldn't possibly have any memory of. But if something tragic was reported to have happened to any of these figments, the event would stick in Margaret P.'s mind, and a little while later she would have herself believing that the thing had happened to somebody in her own immediate family, sometimes even to herself. Albert and Bernadette came to visit one time and reported on the death of Huey the Bird MacIntyre from Dunvegan, who had gone into the hospital for chest x-rays and wasn't allowed to leave because the doctors discovered he was filled up with the cancer. The very next day Margaret P. was creaking back and forth in her chair saying, "God love me, I went into the hospital for chest x-rays and they found out I was full of the cancer." And she cried, tearless and almost soundless, for the rest of the day, while Albert knelt by her chair in agony trying to make her drink rum and milk, and her other son Rollie made circles and covered his ears, and Bridget's father kept bursting into the room and looking at the three of them in disgust and hollering, "For the lova Jesus, Ma! It's Huey the Bird's got the cancer! And he's dead!" And Margaret P. would ask why he was so cruel to her, and he would stomp out again. And Margaret P. would say rosaries on her own behalf for the rest of the night.

Now she was saying them all the time for Bridget, Gerard reported. She was always hearing some new story about such-and-such and inevitably used it to explain to herself why Bridget wasn't there. In anticipation of this, Bridget's mother neglected to say anything about Archie Shearer and Jennifer MacDonnell, but the tragedy came up anyway when Mrs. Boucher, Margaret P.'s old live-in housekeeper, came down from Louisdale for a visit. Mrs. Boucher — Bridget could picture her sitting in a plastic-covered chair brought in from the kitchen, smoking, her tiny feet barely touching the carpet — had let the cat out of the bag regarding Jennifer MacDonnell. You couldn't blame Mrs. Boucher — she loyally came to visit Margaret P. on the seventeenth of every month and was more wizened and saintly than mother Theresa herself. Besides, when somebody died an untimely death, you spoke about it to your friends.

"Olivia Morrison's granddaughter? You knew Olivia Morrison, Margie, she was just from Duck Cove."

"Oh, God love her. Poor Libby."

"No, Libby die in seventy-eight, it was her granddaughter got kill."

"How old was she?"

"I doan know, love. Sixteen? Seventeen? Eighteen? She went to school with Bridget, Joan said."

"Ach. God love her poor dear soul," Margaret P. would say, the rusty wheels in her head turning in all the wrong directions.

That was all it took for Margaret P. to wake up the whole house in the middle of the night, pounding on the wall with her bedpan and saying that she wanted her beads, and she wanted her slender white communion candles lit, and she wanted her three-dimensional picture of Christ at the Last Supper plugged in, and everybody had to kneel and say the first string with her because Bridget Murphy, her own granddaughter, had been shot to death by a boy.

It seemed like, when Bridget started taking care of Margaret P. more and more, they came to like one another less. This was why Bridget couldn't understand Margaret P.'s torment at her absence. Unless it was perhaps just a matter of a disrupted routine, which Margaret P. and also Rollie had always been known to get upset at. Every night without fail, before going to bed, Rollie shambled out of his chair in the corner and went to his mother's room and got the holy water off her dresser. Then he would hand it to her, and she would near-sightedly splash some on him and make the sign of the cross and kiss him good night, and he would put it back. Sometimes he would stand at the dresser for a little while, pressing against it with his fingers and humming a little, until Bridget's father hollered from the living room to get the Christ to bed. Sometimes Rollie would do the same sort of thing halfway up the stairs, leaning over to press his fingers against the next step and humming. This was even more infuriating to Bridget's father than when Rollie lingered in Margaret P.'s room — probably because her father could see him at it — and he would bark three quick times, GET UP THERE, and send Rollie shambling the rest of the way, snorting and mumbling, "Chris' Almighty, hurry up. Chris' Almighty, hurry up, Rollie," to himself.

Rollie pronounced his own name like this: Ro-hee. He referred to himself as either Ro-hee or Him or He. And he called Bridget Bri-het and Bridget's mother Joad. And Gerard was Je-hard, which was pretty close, and Bridget's father was Raw-hurt. He mispronounced everybody's name in some little way, and they had all been listening to him so long that around the house they would take to calling one another by Rollie's names. Gerard used to imitate Rollie at the supper table, sometimes to make them laugh but sometimes almost unconsciously, and say "Joad, where's his tea, Joad, Chris' Almighty, he wants his tea." Guests would stop by for dinner and hear them all impersonating Rollie and not know what was going on.

Rollie was much worse than Margaret P. for wanting things to be the same. Bridget's mother always complained that he was at her every day about Bridget being gone. He had gone into Bridget's room and picked up a stuffed carrot that was on her dresser — from a long-gone oversized Bugs Bunny she'd been given as a baby. And Bridget's mother said Rollie was carrying this carrot around and saying he was looking after it for Bridget. And sometimes when Bridget and her mother were talking on the phone, Rollie would appear and stand there looking at Joan with the carrot tucked under his arm like a newspaper until she held the phone up to his face, and he would say, "Where are you, Bri-het?"

"I'm in Halifax."

"She's in Halifax. It's all right, Ro-hee. When you coming home?"

"Pretty soon."

"Pre-hee soon, pre-hee soon."

"How ya doing anyway, Roland?"

"Say 'Stop it.'"

She would sing-song, "Stop it . . ." and hear him laugh on the other end.

"Stop it . . ." he would prompt.

"Stop it . . . how's my carrot, Rollie?"

"Stopppp it . . ."

"Stoppppp it," she'd sing for him, just as she'd been doing since the age of two.

"There, that's enough for a while," she heard him say, satisfied and moving away from the telephone back to his chair. In the background, she could hear Margaret P. calling "Help me! Help me! Help me!" — her voice getting higher and higher — and Bridget knew as soon as they went to see to her she would curse at them and then pretend they weren't there for a couple of seconds, then spit snot into a Kleenex and throw it at them. She heard the considerable noise of her father moving down the hall to see what in Christ's name she wanted now.

"You must be glad to get away from this madhouse," Bridget's mother said from her end of the line.

Bridget told Gerard about this last phone call, hoping to make him laugh. "She always says that to me, too." He smiled, scratching his face where he was trying to grow a beard. Bridget wondered if the irony had been lost on him, or what. Gerard, as far as she knew, did not have much use for irony.

A little while into the visit, Bridget noticed that she was doing most of the talking — unusual for her. She was telling Gerard stories about their mother, how funny she had been in August, when she was in town to help Bridget. She saw Gerard shift in his chair at the mention of August, and she talked faster. She wanted him to know that it had been funny, that there had been things that kept happening the whole time which were actually funny, and just because she was where she was didn't necessarily mean that things couldn't be funny any more. She wanted very much for Gerard to know that she wasn't going to make him feel uncomfortable or revolted, she wasn't going to start doing things or saying things. She wasn't going to walk over to where he was sitting and lay her head on his lap and ask him to help her. Things were as always. The two of them, sitting and laughing at their family.

Her mother had the greatest time when she was there with Bridget, when Bridget was in the hospital for a real reason. She went to the stores and bought presents for everybody and drank a couple of beer every night with Bernadette while Albert sipped on the non-alcoholic kind — "queer beer," he called it — and told stories to remind them of the things they used to do when they were in their twenties. The night after Bridget's ordeal, Joan went back to Bernadette and Albert's place while Bridget slept off her epidural and proceeded to drink two bottles of wine on top of a couple of rums with Bernadette and her oldest daughter Candace — the only one of eleven children still living nearby. And the next morning Bridget, wakened with a kiss on the cheek, opened her eyes and saw her mother putting down an ugly little plant and smiling palely. Her mother went to confession every Sunday and didn't believe in holding anything back. "Well, I went and got liquored," she told Bridget at once.

"You did!"

"Yes," she said, sitting down and giving the plant a little pat. "I was sick on the drive over here."

"Mother!"

"I had to roll down the window and lean out of the car!" she said, briefly touching her own cheeks with the tips of her fingers.

Albert had been standing in the doorway because he was smoking a cigarette. "Goddammit," he called. "You woulda been proud of your mother. It was just like the old days, when she used to swing on the chandelier up there at the Wandlyn."

"I saw it in a movie," she explained when Bridget looked at her. She sat up straight and smiled out the window at the rooftops, the four of them — Bridget's mother, Bridget, Albert and Bernadette — all being quiet for a time while Joan tried to remember which movie it had been.

"Um, it wasn't Abbot and Costello," she said at last. "Oh! Jerry Lewis! I loved that movie. I loved him. I always wanted to try it after that. That was the only chandelier in town."

While she waited for Bridget to finish speaking with the doctor or the nurses or Babs the social worker, Bridget's mother used to wander around the wards looking for children. She told Bridget about some poor wee thing alone in a crib, crying and crying, and she

walked all over the ward peeping in the rooms until she found it.
There were absolutely no nurses around, she said, so she went over
and picked the poor wee thing up and walked around with it singing
"Mama's Little Baby Loves Shortenin' Bread" until it settled down.
And this baby might have had cancer or cystic fibrosis or holes in its
heart or be HIV positive for all Bridget's mother knew. Bridget's
mother made friends with this other little girl who was about nine
but was only two feet tall and whose legs were all deformed and who
was brain damaged and could hardly speak, she said. Her name was
Charlotte, but she was only one of the many poor wee things her
mother had more or less adopted during that time. Bridget always
imagined her mother strolling through the electric grey corridors,
humming "Mama's Little Baby" to herself, hoping for lepers to kiss.

Mona was in love with Bridget's mother. Bridget didn't know
why, she guessed it was because of the Vaseline. One day in the adult
hospital in a roomful of doctors and nurses and other postpartums,
her mother had offered her a small tube of Vaseline.

"What'll I do with that?"

"Put it on your stitches — Bernadette says it softens them right
up. I'm sure it says something about it on here . . ." She had held the
tube up to her face to read the tiny blue lettering.

"No, it won't say anything about that, Mumma," Bridget said
hastily. Her mother must have thought she felt doubtful when what
she had really meant to convey was that she didn't want to talk about
her stitches in front of all these people. But her mother continued
reading until she saw something that made her titter. She covered
her mouth like a girl.

"Lip Therapy, it says right here!"

Mona had rolled back and forth on her bed upon hearing this,
her face red, with no sound coming out of her. Bridget didn't know
if she should be embarrassed or what — she thought she had been
complaining and expected Mona to nod sympathetically. She realized that she did not know much about Mona at all. She was still
getting used to finding Mona in her room, sometimes lounging on
her bed as she painted her toenails different colours, or sometimes

looking through Bridget's drawers for something new to wear. It was not that Bridget minded this kind of thing, it was just that she wasn't used to it. And there were enough people contemplating her stitches and her lips and all they implied and entailed as it was.

Mona's silent rolling had broken out into horse-like guffaws, and she sat up abruptly, scratching her yin-yang tattoo. The story ended up endearing Bridget's mother to her forever. "I fucking love your mom," she would holler whenever the subject came up. "Your mom is the fucking coolest."

Mostly Mona only talked about her father. It seemed she was obsessed. She would do sit-ups and push-ups in front of Bridget, raving about him all the while. She said she thought he was the devil or at least really, really, really evil. Like, an Evil Force. She would spread her arms and make her eyes wide when she said her father was an Evil Force. Mona never tried to explain to Bridget what it was her father did. Bridget asked her to once and she couldn't. "It's control. And it's, like, the great almighty sanctified privilege of being an asshole. And treating people like shit! Like the shit that comes out of the asshole." This was as far as Mona could go with regard to her father before she started really raving, raving about his eyes and his mouth and his German accent and his second wife and his navy suits. Bridget could not put it together, but she knew she felt horrible listening to Mona tell it. Recently Mona had taken to coming into Bridget's room at around midnight and crawling to her bed and shaking her, even though Bridget was always awake. And when Bridget asked what was wrong, Mona only knelt there with her freckled face all squashed and red, making choking noises. Then she would go away again. It was terrible to see.

The next day Mona would say, "You're fucking great, you know that? I really think you're, like, this angel sent for me. You just sit there and you never say anything." Mona took out her tarot cards and said she was going to teach Bridget what they meant.

"I had an abortion," she said, dealing the cards into the shape of a cross, "and I don't care what people say, I don't think it's that big a deal. And I was raped, too. But that wasn't the same thing about the abortion. Anyway, I'm not a feminist. When is your birthday?"

"May."

"Okay, so you're a Gemini. That makes you . . . I can't remember. I think swords. Anyway, we'll say swords. The Page of Swords, you'll be. Oh! Do you know what I am?" Mona began rummaging through the pack. "I'm a Leo. Leo the lion, no joke. Do you want to see my card?" She rummaged for a few minutes more and finally slapped down a card with a picture of a women who was using both hands either to open or to close a lion's mouth. She said she was going to have the picture tattooed onto her thigh or her back one day.

CHAPTER 3

Alan Voorland was able to take her out on day passes because he qualified as an adult. He was one. He pulled into Tim Horton's at first and said they were going to have dinner there. It was a joke, and funny because they always used to drive to the Tim Horton's in Antigonish in order to get away from town. They would joke about having driven an hour just to sit and smoke and drink coffee.

Alan always spoke as if he were reading the news. "Here I am with my funny friend Bridget Murphy," he said in the restaurant he took her to after the joke about Tim's. "Out on a day pass from the psychiatric ward. Yes indeed. She is somewhat gaunt in appearance but seems in good health overall."

When she first met him, this way of speaking had made her feel special. "Here I am with Bridget Murphy," he would announce as they drove aimlessly around the back roads, stopping to examine the many little family cemeteries. "A fascinating young lady." But Alan found everything fascinating. He was from Guelph and wandered around town examining and exclaiming at everything like an anthropologist. He was a twenty-five-year-old engineer who had been hired by the mill but wasn't sure if he was going to stay. "Do not get me wrong," he used to warn Bridget, staring out over the steering wheel. "This is a wonderful place, a fascinating people with a thriving, unique culture. And yet there is a sadness. A hopelessness about it all. The dependence on welfare, unemployment insurance. The bottle."

"You sound like a newscaster," Bridget said, noticing for the first time.

"I am a mediaphile," Alan acknowledged. "Do you listen to CBC?"

"Radio?"

"Of course."

"Mumma listens to the gardener in the afternoons."

"Good God, this girl needs educating. But then, you're only young."

It was impossible not to feel special. It was also impossible not to feel a little dumb. For the first time she experienced herself and her surroundings as something other than commonplace. For Alan they were positively alien. He wanted to hear stories about Bridget's Gramma.

"And what do they call her?"

"Margaret P."

"Mahr-gar-het Pee," he repeated. "And what does she say?"

"When?"

"You know — what's one of those things you told me she says?"

"She says 'Mait-el on your heart.'"

"And what does that mean?"

"I guess it just means bless your heart. That's when she's in a good mood. Sometimes she'll call me to her and give me twenty dollars out of her purse."

"What about when she isn't in a good mood?"

"She'll tell ya to suck her hole."

"No, come on, in Gaelic."

"I don't know." Bridget taught him a few curses. Alan asked if she was speaking in Irish Gaelic or Scottish Gaelic and Bridget didn't know.

She met him because she had worked at the auditorium for concerts and plays, and Alan had gone to every one of them for something to do. He talked to her because he was lonely and knew hardly anyone but the mill people. He was as interesting to her as she was to him because he talked more, even when sober, than any other man she knew. He talked just for the sake of talking, using words that weren't even necessary to get the meaning across. He may as well have had a horn coming out of his forehead. Everyone else she knew, Mark, the guys at Dan Sutherland's, spoke briefly, as briefly as possible, trying to make it seem as though they hadn't really said anything at all and you were the one making unfounded inferences.

Alan would take her to his apartment after the shows and play Bessie Smith for her and read her the letters he was writing to his girlfriend. He lived in the Springdale Apartments — the only apartment buildings in town — where many of what her mother called Welfare People lived. And if it wasn't welfare people, it was people like Alan, who were from away. Mark's friend, George Matheson, had a little Acadian girlfriend who in point of fact lived in the basement of Alan's building and worked at the Co-op. Because she had her own apartment, her place became a favoured place to drink. Even over Dan Sutherland's, since you always had to be worried about not breaking anything or throwing up on the carpet. So for a while Bridget and Mark went to Chantal's on the weekends, but Daniel and Stephen and the rest of them showed up rarely because George thought they were fags. Bridget actually preferred Daniel's place, and this was one of the first things she and Mark fought about. At Chantal's, there were other girlfriends, none of whom knew each other but felt they had to talk to one another anyway. At Dan Sutherland's, she had been the only girl except, sometimes, for Heidi, who had been stringing Stephen Cameron along for the last year and would drop by every now and again just to prod his hopes back to life.

So this was why Bridget felt funny in Alan's apartment — the antithesis of Chantal's down below — with its enormous stereo and Degas prints and Alan's typewriter collection, which he had actually lugged all the way from Guelph. That was why Bridget felt funny, but that was not what Alan thought.

"Here I am with a seventeen-year-old in my apartment, and it has just occurred to her that I may very well be planning to rub my fat hairy body all over her little smooth one." He was trying to yank the cork out of a previously opened bottle of wine and smiling down at it.

"No, no," she assured him.

"My God, I just read you my letters to my girlfriend. I would have to be quite the cad."

Alan's letters sounded exactly like he spoke. Descriptive of his surroundings, almost to the point of being scientific. Bridget wondered if his anthropological interest would extend to Chantal and her shit-box downstairs, with its Jack Daniels banner on the window and the strobe light and George's amp and guitar in the corner. She thought it probably would. And what about upstairs, on the top floor, where there was a midget named Tina who often used to call upon Chantal to babysit for her, and sometimes, when her two children were asleep, would come down to join their parties. George and the guys made fun of her when she left because she was so much older and wore such tight clothes and had so many tattoos covering her little body. They called her Troll. One time Tina brought her children down to show everybody. She couldn't walk well to begin with, and seeing her struggling across the threshold with a full-sized baby made Bridget sure that the woman was going to topple over when she took her next step. But what surprised everyone most was her also-full-sized three-year-old, Christa, who looked like something out of a television commercial, with gold curls and round blue eyes, wearing an innocent white nightgown with angels on it. The child was hyperactive and ran around the apartment wanting to climb on everybody.

"She takes 'er out of me, that one does," Tina said, sitting down at the kitchen table. And to all the boys' — and the girls', too, to be fair — horror, Tina wearily pulled up her tank top and began to feed the infant with one of her little boobies. And she continued to complain about Christa, who had "found her friggin legs" and was always running away from Tina, who wouldn't be taller than her for much longer and who couldn't chase after her, what with the bad hip.

In any event, the last time Bridget had spoken to Chantal, she

said Christa had fallen out of the window of Tina's top floor apartment and lay there on the grass for a few moments in, perhaps, surprise, before getting up and heading back inside to meet her weeping, limping mother on the stairs. Completely undamaged. "God
looks after drunks and small children!" was what Mark had to say
about that. Of course Children's Aid came and took Christa and the
baby anyway. All this before Alan's arrival on the second floor.

Bridget's friendship with Alan Voorland was such that they told
stories about themselves to one another. It took Bridget a little while
to get the hang of this, and so in the beginning Alan did the most of
it. He told her about his intelligent and interesting friends and all
the quirky, whimsical adventures they had together. He took out a
notebook and said it was full of character sketches he had written
about all his interesting friends. He read some of them to her. There
was a girl named Quentin who bought all her clothes at Kensington
Market and wrote haiku all the time. "Literally, all the time," Alan
stressed. He closed the notebook and said that once he had thought
he could write a book, what with knowing so many interesting and
original people, but when he tried, all he ended up with were pages
and pages of overly descriptive character sketches. "I can't help that,"
he said. "It's the little things that fascinate me."

"Like me," Bridget said. Wittily, she thought.

In the restaurant, Alan tried to get her to tell him the story of the
last few months. She did it easily, picking out the little details she
knew he would find funny — like a nurse who gave her a poem
about Jesus walking at your side throughout your lifetime and the
doctor who wore brown socks and sandals and said that he didn't
like to be called Doctor. She told about her mother being hung over
the morning after and hanging out the car window. He loved that.
The thing he laughed about most was her breasts. She called it the
Tit Fiasco. Having been released for the long weekend to Albert and
Bernadette, she ran out of medication for her breasts. What happened was that she went to a pharmacy to beg for a refill because she

was in terrible pain and they were dripping. She jumped from foot to foot feeling like some kind of prescription junkie while the pharmacist phoned the doctor who didn't like to be called Doctor. In the hospital, the doctor had assured Bridget that he would let her have one more round, but now that the pharmacist was calling, he suddenly changed his mind and said it would be better not to give her any more.

"Well, what am I supposed to do?" Bridget had pleaded.

"You have to understand," the pharmacist said, his face contorting. When Bridget looked back on the event, she realized his face had been contorting in pain, and that was because he was looking at Bridget, seeing what she felt. "If you keep taking the medication, they'll just keep filling up and going down again, you'll never dry up."

"I don't *care*," said Bridget, hopping. Wet circles coming through her sweater.

"I'm sorry," he said.

Bridget went down the aisle in the drug store. If she had been one of Alan's fascinating and unique Guelph friends she might have overturned the shelves of tampons and napkins and condoms and shampoo. Instead she took a taxi to Albert and Bernadette's, and Bernadette, who had been a nurse, wrapped bandages tightly around Bridget's upper body until she looked like a burn victim. Then she made Bridget drink down a glass of apple juice and Epsom salts and sent her to bed, which was precisely where Bridget wanted to be. She slept for half an hour and then she had diarrhea. She related all this to Alan as amusingly as she could.

"Then I was leaking out of the other end," she finished. Alan was in tears.

"Didn't you know Epsom salts are a laxative?"

"No, I was totally not expecting it. I thought it was God again, adding insult to injury."

CHAPTER 4

Alan told her that he wanted to go back to Guelph. The place that had once been so fascinating had rapidly lost its rustic charm and begun to do bad things to him, he said. He was getting fatter and fatter with no gym to work out at, and the shifts at the mill were completely fucking up his internal clock. And the guys he worked with on the platform were either drunk or hung over all the time and were going to kill somebody soon. And the overweight woman who worked at the liquor store who he used to flirt with (Bridget knew who he meant, Margaret Ann MacDougal) kept giving him dirty looks because he was buying so much scotch and because he couldn't be bothered pretending to find her attractive any more. And she wore glasses that magnified her eyes to twice the appropriate size and made her look as if she were perpetually astonished at everything Alan said to her. It unsettled him. The whole place was beginning to unsettle him. Alan straightened up and said in his protective newscaster's voice, "There's nothing there worth staying for. I could see that as soon as you took off. You were the one bright light." He laughed.

"I'm a bright light all right."

"I miss Guelph. I never thought I'd say that. I miss my friends and going for weekends in Toronto and to our cottages on Georgian Bay. I guess I miss Deanna quite a bit, too."

"Yeah." His girlfriend.

"You should apply for school out there."

"School out there?"

"What else are you going to do?"

"I don't know."

"You could come up with me," he said. "Apply for January."

Bridget looked around the restaurant. Pub, really — too hip to be called a restaurant. All the waitresses were bouncy and alive, wearing shorts of all things. To think of her and Alan and Deanna and all of Alan's cool buddies who worked in television and were photographers and played in rock and roll bands, real rock and roll bands, not George and Mark mangling Aerosmith in Chantal's living room. She had this thing she did now, cultivated at the hospital. She never tried to answer questions that she had no answers for. She never tried to make up any suitable answers.

"I'm worried about you, you know," he said after a while. He was struggling with his newscaster's tone. He wasn't sure if it should be there or not. "What you're going to do."

"Did you hear about the girl who got shot?" she said.

"At my favourite donut shop? I guess to God. That was one of the things that got me thinking about going home."

"Really?"

"The field behind the shop were it happened. My apartment looks out over it. Gah. And it all yellow and dead and scarcely even September."

"They don't shoot people in Guelph?"

"It's not so close. Not right under my nose like that. If I hadn't been at work, I could have stood at my window and watched the whole thing. Oh, I want to go home," he said, loudly and suddenly, not like he was reading the news.

Bridget felt badly for him. He used to narrate happy stories of himself and all his friends on Georgian Bay — tanned sons and daughters of lawyers and accountants. And a girl he used to sleep with who turned a whole jar of peanut butter upside down on his penis one time. He was still friends with her, he said. He was still friends with all his old lovers. And he and all his friends would go and see concerts and baseball and hockey games in Toronto. He made it sound like so much fun, and it probably was.

They sat quietly for quite a few minutes while Alan struggled with his voice.

"Which reminds me," he finally said. "Your boyfriend has been calling."

"You?"

"Yeah."

"Sorry," she said after a moment. Why the hell did you ever go out with him anyway, he always used to ask. And the only thing she could say was, "Oh well, it wasn't always like that. You know, like at first he asked me to the formal and gave me a corsage and stuff." "Fucking hell," Alan said. "You're only seventeen. Corsage. I keep forgetting. I swear to God." This was the time when they were sitting in his car on top of Creignish Mountain, peering through the windshield and into the black woods. Alan produced a case of beer, and Bridget knew. He was tired of driving around the back roads telling stories and educating her about things. She had told him all there was to know about her, everything of current relevance. He was getting her drunk, and he was getting himself drunk. There was nothing wrong with it. "Here I am in love with pregnant teenager Bridget Murphy," he tittered, lighting a smoke. It was a Ford Escort — Alan later enjoyed referring to it as The Car of Shame — and she rubbed the spots where the knobs and handles and arm rests had jammed into her. Bridget was pretty sure about what Alan meant when he said "in love," so she wasn't worried about that. But there was a disappointment, inevitable. She knew that he was good, that Alan Voorland was a good guy in every way, but she also saw that he could not help being pleased with himself. And later he could not help feeling bad, but even the guilt must have been a form of pleasure for someone like him.

"And what does he say?" she asked after a while.

"You know what he says. It must be all the same kind of shit he used to say to you." Alan pursed his lips — a Gerard gesture. It was all too sordid. Tabloid news. Alan couldn't wait to go home.

Chantal wanted to marry George Matheson, Bridget remembered. Probably she still did. When she was at work the guys would play in her apartment and make up songs about her with titles like "Marry Me You Prick" and imitate her accent while they sang. Chantal took Bridget into her room one time. They both had water pistols filled with Jack Daniels and every now and again would squirt some into the other's mouth. Chantal was very aggressive about this and sometimes caught Bridget unawares, like when she was yawning.

"I just want to get away from those bastards for a while," she said, talking about the boys who were all drunk and making fun of her to her face. "Luh," she commanded, pointing with one hand to the fingers on her other hand, and then to her neck. "George gave me this ring, this ring, and this chain. There's another chain somewheres else too — silver. I don't know what the fuck his problem is. I say, luh, asshole, I'm done school, I work. You're almost done school, and Mark can get you on at Home Hardware. This is what people do, they get jobs and get married. He goes, Oh well, we're kinda young. What, you see old people getting married a lot? Senior citizens. Yeah, they really get married a lot." Bridget opened her mouth to say something and Chantal shot Jack Daniels into it — five quick squirts. Bridget was bothered because Chantal was acting as if they were confidantes, and Chantal made her uncomfortable. She was always talking about weddings and babies and stuffed animals. George had given her an entire menagerie of stuffed animals for every occasion, and they were all lined up on her bed. So many girls were like that that Bridget scarcely had any friends who were girls at all except for Heidi — so aggressively friendly in her self-absorbed manner that you were friends with her whether you meant to be or not. But even though Heidi had her own accumulation of stuffed animals and chains and rings, she did not seem to embody the stuff the way Chantal did — the philosophy behind it all, if you could call it that. The problem was that Chantal was not harmless. She sat cross-legged on her bed in her fuzzy pink room, sucking in her cheeks and thinking about George, about how to get him to marry her.

"Do you know what he said? Do you know what he said, the frig?

He said he wouldn't marry me even if I got pregnant. So that's out. Bastard's got no religion." She rested her face in her hand, scratching it briefly with frosted pink nails of intimidating length. Bridget couldn't help but think that no matter how George laughed with his friends, and no matter how many songs he made up about her, it wouldn't be long before the hollow cheeks and the dark French eyes got the better of him. Bridget had heard about Chantal and the kind of things she did. George had been going out with Darlene MacEachern before Chantal moved to town from Cheticamp and methodically terrorized Darlene into stepping aside. These were just rumours, but the rumours were of phone calls at three in the morning, a number of unsavoury items left morningly on the MacEachern's doorstep, and an actual encounter of some kind in the girl's bathroom at a dance at the vocational school. Darlene was the daughter of one of the managers at the mill and could hardly stand against such tactics. Chantal told Bridget that this was how things were done back home and went on to tell her a story about one time in grade ten when she had waited for a rival after school with a pair of scissors and then jumped out and grabbed a handful of the girl's hair, yanked the girl towards her so as to get hold of an even bigger handful, and then cut all the hair off as close to the scalp as she could manage. The only thing to be done was for the girl to have the rest of her head shaved, and every time she passed her in the hall afterwards, Chantal would shout the French equivalent of "Baldie!" and she and all her friends would laugh.

"I used to be best friends with that girl," Chantal reflected, picking up one of her teddy bears and giving it a squeeze.

Bridget told Mark all the things Chantal said to her whenever she dragged her into her bedroom at the parties. She said she thought Chantal was a loony.

"I think it's great," Mark said. "She's got balls, fighting for her man and shit. Would you do that?"

"I don't think a person should have to."

They had ended up talking about what Chantal did to Darlene MacEachern because Darlene's younger brother had killed himself that week, and they'd started out talking about that. This was what everyone was talking about — his father being so high up at the mill. Darlene MacEachern's brother had driven out to Point Tupper and parked at a place where a lot of high school kids came at night. It overlooked both the water and the mill, and so at night the white and yellow and red lights of the latter would twinkle sentimentally off the former. But this had been in the afternoon, in wintertime, and he had brought all his grandmother's painkillers for her cancer, which he swallowed with Orange Big 8. Everybody talked about how no one was expecting it because this boy had been captain of the hockey team and student council something-or-other and all that. And Mark had said he thought pills were cowardly, but Bridget couldn't see anything cowardly about killing oneself in any manner. Because, she said, whenever a person risks his life for whatever reason, everyone says how brave he is. But when someone actually takes it, he's called a coward. That made no sense.

"What makes no sense," said Mark, killing the conversation, "is why we all don't put ourselves out of our misery all at once like a big fucking Jonestown."

Killing conversations was something Mark had begun to do. Even though Bridget had come to recognize this as the first sign of drunken nastiness to come, she still had no idea how to go about nipping it in the bud. At parties he would become angry with her for something she had said or done, some insensitive comment to George or whoever, and ignore her for hours. And then, just as she was in the middle of a conversation with somebody else, holler across the room wanting to know why she insisted going on about something she knew absolutely nothing about? Why didn't she stick to talking about Chimney Corner — the little bitty community where her father's relatives were all from? Even though Bridget didn't understand why in the world he was hollering about Chimney Corner, her conversation would keel over. Not just hers, but everybody's, which Bridget didn't think was fair. So for considerable minutes everyone sat glumly contemplating their dead conversations to the music of Pink Floyd. Mark lit a smoke, looking at them all, drunk enough to feel that he had accomplished something important. He had showed them. This was when things were getting bad.

When Bridget got around to telling all this to Alan Voorland, he could only reiterate his surprise at how young she was. "He's just a mean drunk. How could you think you were doing something wrong when he was just a mean drunk?"

"Because he never used to be a mean drunk, to me."

She told Alan about how one night Chantal had yanked Bridget into her teddy-stuffed room to talk about marrying George and without warning turned her beady dark eyes up to her and said, "So what about you and Mark?"

"Eh?"

"When are you guys getting married? I see he's started ignoring you at the parties. That's a sure sign!" She threw back her delicate head and laughed. And the crazy thing was that when she and Mark were walking home in the snow and she was telling him about this and laughing, he had started yelling at her again for always making fun of Chantal.

"But you guys always make fun of Chantal," she protested.

"But we're not fucking mean-spirited about it."

"Yes, you are," she said. And Mark proceeded to lecture her about how Chantal was a nice fucking girl from whom Bridget could learn a thing or two.

"You've gone insane," Bridget said before going inside for the night. And she didn't talk to him after that, not for weeks, and that was when the phone started ringing at three or four in the morning, or sometimes she'd be on her way to bed and have almost all the lights turned out when she'd spot the double reflection of his glasses outside the front door.

"That's gotta be kinda scary," Alan observed.

"No, no," she said. "I always knew it was him."

CHAPTER 5

She was in the kitchen baking an angel food cake for Kelly, a girl on the ward who was turning fifteen. When she was admitted, the doctor or the nurses or somebody asked Bridget's mother about what kind of things Bridget liked to do, and Bridget's mother said that Bridget liked to bake desserts. So the psychiatric nurses forced her into the kitchen to make a cake for Kelly, saying it would be nice to get one from someone on the ward. Bridget thought it was actually quite a sadistic gesture because Kelly was a scarcely recovered anorexic, having only been admitted a month ago, who cried every time she was made to sit down to a meal. The preferred therapy if you were an anorexic on the ward seemed to be that you either ate regularly from the uniform plastic trays that were sent up from the cafeteria, or else you were forced to stay in bed, in pyjamas, day and night, with a needle in your arm and perhaps a tube up your nose if things didn't soon improve. To add insult to injury, these girls were never allowed to go to the bathroom for an hour after eating unless accompanied by a staff, even if they really had to.

Bridget was lucky that she was not anorexic, because pretty much all of her spare time was spent in the bathroom waiting to not be constipated any more. She would come out and trudge down the hall to the TV room, feeling as if she possessed a bum full of concrete, and Gabby would come dancing up from behind and put her arm around her.

"How you doing, me love me dear me darling?"

"Shitty."

"Language. Missing your mom?"

"Constipated."

"Aw. That's what's got you bummed out?" Bridget rolled her eyes and Gabby realized she'd made a joke and began laughing her head off and ran to tell the other staff on duty. Bridget asked for Epsom salts, remembering their unwarranted effectiveness on the day of the Tit Fiasco, but was refused. This was aggravating. Why? Why would they refuse her Epsom salts? It was not as if she had asked for morphine. Hauling her hundred pound arse around the kitchen, Bridget had the feeling that the ward and its methods were as arbitrary as the days were long.

She had separated six eggs into two different bowls when Byron strolled into the kitchen, even though the staff had said that no other patient was allowed in there that afternoon except for Bridget. He walked up to her and stuck his face in the bowls to see what was there.

"Chicken embryos!" he said. "Yum! Yum! I just love chicken embryos! Don't you love chicken embryos?"

"I'm telling," Bridget said to him unconvincingly, picking up the bowl of whites and commencing to beat them into fluff with a whisk. "Not allowed in here."

"What are you making anyway?"

"Chicken embryo soup."

"What I've always wondered," he said, scratching his acne and talking in a loud self-conscious voice, "is how chickens can lay eggs without the rooster being around."

"The eggs and the chicks aren't the same thing," Bridget said with authority. In reality, she wasn't sure herself and had to think about it.

"I know that," Byron said, pointing his protruding front teeth at her and looking offended. Byron was always telling everybody how he had been tested and discovered to have an IQ of 200 — which meant nothing to Bridget — and that, he said, was why he was in here. He frightened people, he said, with his intellect. So if anybody ever suggested to Byron that he didn't know something they did, he would get very angry and sometimes do weird things. Bridget assumed this was likely the real reason he was in here.

"I mean, women have eggs," continued Bridget, figuring it out. "They're not embryos, they're eggs. All female animals have eggs, right? It's just a matter of whether they get fertilized or not. The difference is that chicken's eggs come right out of them, and if they're fertilized they hatch, and if they're unfertilized they just sit there. So one day, I guess, somebody probably saw that all these eggs weren't hatching into chicks and . . . decided to eat them," she finished. Byron tried to kiss her. He had thought she was talking dirty, she supposed.

She pushed him away with the bowl of whites that was between them, not yet foamy enough to keep from sloshing onto Byron's white dress shirt — the only kind he ever wore.

"Oh, fuck off with this," she said, because he was always doing such things with either her or Mona — the oldest girls on the ward. Mona made blood really pour from his nose once in the bathtub room because the two of them were having a seance in there and he had tried to touch what Mona liked to call her taco. And Mona said she had waited to see if he knew what to do with it and soon found he didn't, and so that was when she made the blood flow. Mona got all her privileges taken away for two weeks on top of an hour in the quiet room, where she choreographed a little dance recital for herself to all her favourite Tina Turner songs.

Byron sat down and began tapping his fingers on the table in a gesture of nonchalance. He was smiling and his lips were trembling and he was crying. He was so naked it made Bridget sick to look at him. "You're not even supposed to be here," she said, going to get the sugar.

"You guys are such incredible teases," he said, shaking his head.

"Why? Because we breathe?"

"You know why," he said, acne blazing. He really believed she did.

Mona heard them in the hall and came bounding in to see what was going on. She began to laugh at Byron because he was crying,

and she told him that he was always crying, that he'd cried when she
hit him, and any guy who cried every time he made an unsuccessful
attempt to get his rocks off was pretty much through before he began, or something to that effect. And Bridget, who could feel something unpleasant welling up every time she looked at him, rejoined
something to the effect of "Yeah," surprising herself.

Some other people on the ward heard Byron barking back at
them and came to see what was going on. Even Kelly, whose cake
was supposed to be a surprise. Everybody watched as Mona and
Bridget commenced to bait and berate Byron with violent truths
about the way he looked, acted and thought. Byron was a less-than-
formidable opponent because his every response seemed to have
nothing to do with the matter at hand. He would say things like,
"You think you know me? Well, nobody knows me! Nobody really
knows me at all!"

"Thank Jesus for that," Bridget said, making everybody laugh.

And the thing was, Byron was just sitting there, his acne pulsat-
ing and his smile getting stranger and stranger, listening to this ridi-
cule being heaped on him and the uncannily malicious sound of
children's laughter ringing in his ears. He had stopped crying but
kept tapping his long fingers against the table, smiling and smiling
and saying they didn't know him.

It was at this point that Bridget had a revelation — he was enjoying it. He was enjoying it because it was attention. Bridget and
Mona were heaping not abuse but attention on him, and all the people who were laughing at him were, in fact, paying attention to him.
This is what it was. She knew exactly what to say.

"Nobody is irresistibly intrigued by or attracted to you or the way
you think," was what she said. "Not in the remotest possible way."
Byron quit smiling then. He was not crying and was not smiling,
and Bridget experienced a queasy feeling of accomplishment. Byron
coiled himself up and appeared ready to do something weird when
Gabby came dancing authoritatively in and made them all disperse.
Except for Bridget, who went back to making her chicken embryo

soup. So there was nothing for her to do then but sift the sugar into the flour.

Mona decided she liked it. She said Bridget was showing progress and told her that the two of them were going to have many great adventures together. Mona was always talking about going back to Florida, even though she would get arrested if she did. She wanted Bridget to go to Florida with her, as though Bridget's presence would somehow annul the danger. Bridget was some kind of good luck saint, she said. "Doesn't say a word for two months," she kept saying, "and then crucifies some poor schmuck in the kitchen." The blood-thirsty pagan in her could do nothing but applaud, and the more Mona thought about the incident, the more it appealed to her. It made her think that Bridget, in a more benign way than her father, represented some kind of powerful psychic force.

The doctors liked it, too. Bridget had finally done something. Something odd and concrete and cruel. She had reached out to a fellow human being, grabbed hold of a vulnerable extremity, and given it a good yank. Solomon called her to her office for the first time in weeks and wanted to know, "What was it about Byron at that particular moment?"

"I dunno," said Bridget. She was famous for "I dunno."

"From what I hear, you were quite vicious."

"Oh, no," said Bridget.

"Perhaps he reminded you of your boyfriend."

"No, no," said Bridget. "Not at all. Everybody thinks I'm mad at him, but I'm not."

"No?"

"No."

"Then what are you?"

"I'm not. I'm nothing. I'm just not . . ."

"In love with him?"

"Right."

"Indifferent."

"Yep."

"But not to Byron."

"Most of the time I am."

"What happened this time?"

"He was just being so irritating. He was so there. He invites it."

"How?"

"He leaves himself open. It's like someone lying down in the middle of the road just to make people stop and look at him."

"And you decided to run right over him instead."

"There ya go," said Bridget. Taking over her metaphors, the woman was. It was uncomfortable, talking to Solomon. It made her feel like she wanted to go. But she didn't want to feel this way because she had come to know that as soon as you start thinking you want to go, what always happens is that people you didn't even suppose were paying attention all of a sudden decide they can't live without you. Or that you can't live without them. So you have to be restrained.

Solomon just looked at her. It struck Bridget as being a particularly transparent psychiatrist's trick. The doctor was sitting in a position which Bridget's mother would have said was unladylike. Whenever Bridget sat like that, her mother always threatened to send her to finishing school. And because Bridget's chair was lower than Solomon's, she could see up Solomon's woollen skirt. For some reason this didn't undermine the doctor's air of authority one jot, but Bridget wondered how someone as sexually keyed-up as Byron typically responded to it. She thought it must be a terrible torment to be a boy, to be thrown into turmoil by the sight of something as banal as Solomon's sturdy rayon underpants. Bridget looked out the office window, waiting for Solomon to finish looking at her. The doctor, who was sitting in front of her desk, reached behind her to pick up a file.

"I don't know if this should worry me or not, this episode."

"No, no," said Bridget, trying to sound soothing.

She picked with uncharacteristic daintiness through the file. Actually, Solomon often gestured daintily, but it always struck Bridget as being uncharacteristic of her.

"It seems very all-of-a-sudden, but I suppose it constitutes a breakthrough of some sort. Bridget, you've been here since . . . late August. Dr. Rhys suspected postpartum depression. She found you to be . . . apathetic. After . . . The Birth," Solomon finished significantly. Another psychiatrist trick. The springing of harsh truths upon the unsuspecting patient.

"Yes," said Bridget.

"Are you still apathetic?"

"Oh — I dunno — who cares?" said Bridget. "Ha, ha."

"Do you think much? About it? The Birth?"

"Oh, I dunno. Now and then."

"And what do you think?"

"Well," Bridget straightened up. "It struck me that, for an event that everybody claims is so natural, the most natural thing in the world, it didn't seem natural at all."

"No?"

"Nope."

"And what did it seem like?"

"It seemed like a joke someone was playing. And when it didn't seem like that it reminded me of a movie."

"Which movie?"

Bridget made a quick decision not to cite *Rosemary's Baby*. "*Aliens*," she said.

"Ah," said Solomon. Then she admitted she had never seen that particular film. "The body is invaded, I gather, by some foreign entity?"

"An alien," said Bridget, "and it comes smashing out of your chest and . . . kills everybody."

"Including its host?" the doctor asked with excitement.

"Yes, but it's just a movie."

Doctor Solomon closed the file and smiled at Bridget. She seemed somewhat exhilarated. "I think I'm encouraged," she said. "You're opening up and expressing yourself." Bridget sat up, instinctively, at the praise. If Byron had been there, she could have given him a good kick just to reinforce the doctor's pleasure at her progress. Solomon seemed to make a decision right then and there that she had perhaps only been toying with up until now. She leapt from her leather chair and rolled a TV/VCR that had been sitting off to one side over to Bridget, positioning it directly in front of her. She turned it on and the volume was much too high, the roar of static filling the room, deafening, blanketing every other noise like snow blankets a landscape.

"Sorry," shouted Solomon. She pressed play on the VCR which meant that the tape she was going to show Bridget was already in the machine, ready to roll. "Recognize that person?" she said.

It was Bridget, of course, during the preliminary interview with Solomon and the social worker. The Friday before the Tit Fiasco. Oblivious to the fact that she was being taped. The oversized mirror obscuring almost an entire wall — she had scarcely noticed it at the time.

She looked terrible, but this was mostly due to the stark fluorescent lighting in the room, turning everything the usual hospital electric grey. She did not understand how they could expect anyone to talk in that room, to open up, as Solomon might say. You feel so exposed under all that light that the last thing you want to do is open up. What you want is to scuttle into the air duct like a beetle. This was what she remembered, looking at herself.

And she was awfully flabby, if not fat. When she sat down, her breasts looked almost poised to perform a dance on her protruding stomach. She remembered that she had not been wearing a bra for the interview because Bernadette was out buying her new ones, bigger ones, the old ones being intolerable, her breasts were so sore. She remembered that she had come directly from the adults' hospital down the street and had put on jeans and a sweater for the event. But she still had felt, somehow, as if she was in her nightgown. And now Bridget saw that she had looked like she was still wearing a nightgown, too, somehow.

And her hair hadn't been brushed because, she remembered, every time she brushed it, it simply came out.

And, watching herself on the screen, she understood now why the volume had been turned up so high. So that Solomon — who had probably been watching the tape earlier, maybe with some of the staff present for input — could hear Bridget's sparse responses.

"Doesn't seem like the same person, does it?" said Solomon, encouragement of some kind in her voice.

Even though the social worker was supposed to be employed by the hospital — unlike Babs, who worked for children's services — Bridget had only spoken to this woman, surreally named Sylvia Plath, twice since arriving on the ward. This interview was one of those times, and since then Bridget was given no inkling as to what actual purpose Sylvia Plath was supposed to serve, other than this. All she knew was that during the interview Sylvia Plath had taken the role of questioner, and then Bridget only saw her one other time, breezing by to interview Kelly, newly arrived. On the television set, she asked Bridget who the prime minister of Canada was and to recite some of the alphabet backward. When Bridget got to S, Sylvia Plath said she could stop and then asked if she could recite the alphabet backward again, this time skipping every three letters. Bridget looked as though she were about to give it a try but then told Sylvia Plath that she probably could but would rather not at that point in time. Sylvia Plath looked at her for a moment to see if she would change her mind, and then said fine, she didn't have to. Bridget was later to learn that they subjected every new patient to this kind of thing in order to find out how well they were able to concentrate. Solomon stood in the background.

From the screen, Sylvia Plath's voice said, "Dr. Rhys suggested to us that you might need to take some time off, now that it's all over with. . . . How would you like to stay down here as an in-patient for a while, after the long weekend?"

"Okey-doke," the unbrushed person said.

"That way," she went on, as if the patient needed convincing, "you'll have someone to listen to you whenever you feel you need it."

"You don't have to listen to me," the person said generously.

"You don't understand," Dr. Solomon spoke up, the fluorescent lighting doing nothing to diminish her as it did Bridget. Just as Bridget would never have gotten away with Solomon's sitting position. "That's what I'm here for. I want to listen to you."

The person looked up, chewing on her bottom lip. Bridget thought that she looked all worn out. Wrung out. She said, "If somebody was listening to me, I don't know what I'd do. I'd probably start lying to them," and then she looked down again. "Ha, ha," she added after some moments of Sylvia Plath and the doctor's silence.

What Bridget remembered about this whole thing was guilt. She felt bad. She was in a room with two adults asking her questions. She had done something wrong. She hadn't washed for a couple of days. She was seventeen years old. She had been bleeding into a nice, thick hospital napkin which had to be changed every hour. It was not like a period. She was bleeding and bleeding and bleeding and bleeding. Steady, for days. Blood had to be the guiltiest thing there was. It came out and it kept coming. It was like The Birth. "I'm sorry," were the first words she had said after that. And that's what her body had said too, and was still saying.

It seemed like, even if you didn't want it to, or even if you paid no attention to it whatsoever, life, existence, whatever it was, carried on and it carried you with it. Like your body, it was indifferent to you. That's what Bridget thought. Her body was part of life and life was life and always took you along for the ride and you never had any say. You can build a nice little house on the shore and a tidal wave will come and eat it up. You can lie down on your bed, as Bridget remembered doing on her fourteenth birthday, and say, All right. This is horrible. I'm going to die now. But pretty soon your stomach will start growling and you'll begin to think about the leftover lasagne in the fridge whether you want to or not. Whether you want to or not. God could make a sign for all the souls about to be born unto the Earth to take under advisement: "Whether you want to or not."

But perhaps even then you didn't have a choice.

And all the people who went to see Mother Theresa that day had signs that said: Choose Life — as if you could ever do anything but.

For some reason all of this reminded Bridget of a joke her dead Irish grandfather used to tell, particularly on Sundays, because those were the days when his wife Margaret P. would be trying to get everybody to think of God and the devil and the state of their souls. And Grampa, whose name was Peter Joseph Pat, used to stick his long purple-veined nose in her face and say: "Do women have souls, do you think?" And Bridget, pious and fearful, would of course answer: "Yes." In response to which old Peter Joseph Pat would ask: "Why, do you think?" And Bridget, all atremble and being laughed at by her family, who had heard the joke a million times, would say she didn't know.

And the punch line was: "So they can be dammed!"

Everybody else would laugh, but Peter Joseph Pat had been one of those old men who thinks that the funniest thing he can do is to behave very gravely towards children, as if nothing is really that funny to him at all. Bridget was maybe twelve before she figured out that his serious disposition was just a joke he had been making at her expense, and before then she had never been able to reconcile the sombre old fart with the stories that her father and uncle used to tell — about him hiding Margaret P.'s rum on her, or the time he had convinced eight-year-old Albert that the only known cure for the chickenpox he had contracted was to go out to the hen house and collect a bowl of dung, which was to be scrambled with a fresh egg and eaten immediately.

Of course, there were people like Darlene MacEachern's brother, people who chose not to be carried along by life with everybody else like floating dandelion seeds in the summer. But Bridget got the feeling that at some point even such decisive risk-takers as this were thwarted. That maybe you just died and became food for worms and then food for grass and then food for cows and then food for people and maybe somehow at that point you found yourself out of oblivion and floating, like a dandelion seed on a summer's breeze, back down the birth canal again. Which would be fair for people like Jennifer MacDonnell, who presumably hadn't wanted to die in the first place, but not such good news for someone like Darlene MacEachern's brother. Whose name, Bridget remembered, was Kenneth. Kenneth MacEachern.

Bridget had dreamt about Kenneth MacEachern, which was funny because she wasn't even sure what he looked like. He was one of those people you recognized from school but could never put the face to the name. If anyone pointed him out to you, you would say, Oh, yes . . . *him*! *That's* Kenneth MacEachern. But no one had ever done that for Bridget and now no one ever would. So Bridget's dreaming mind probably just made a composite, perhaps out of every boy she'd ever seen at school whose name she didn't know.

What she always dreamt was that she was separating eggs into two bowls, eggs into bowls, that was mostly it. And when she went to separate the very last egg, she discovered there was no yolk inside the shell — it was all white. Sometimes she'd wake up at that point in great distress, and then at other times she'd try to rectify the situation by putting the white in with the rest of the whites and then putting the empty shell in with the yolks, as if to substitute. In a sort of panic she would beat the yolks together in hopes that the shell would blend in with them, only it didn't — you could see the jagged little fragments floating in the frothy yellow. And sometimes she would wake up then. She had these dreams on and off for quite a while after the incident in the kitchen with Byron before Kenneth MacEachern finally made his appearance. She was standing there beating the shell in with the yolks maniacally, beating them and beating them, and finally Kenneth MacEachern — sitting at the end of the table and tapping his fingers — told her that there was nothing to worry about anyway. Because you didn't need yolks for an angel food cake. And after that Bridget didn't have the dream at all any more. She barely slept, in any event.

CHAPTER 6

Mona got out. It was not a big deal — once you had racked up enough points to be allowed to go unaccompanied up to the Teen Lounge, the world was, conceivably, your oyster. You could hop into the elevator and who was to say where you might end up? Everybody did it. Bridget herself had been known to wander down to the gift shop and pick up a couple of Mars bars and a *National Lampoon* when she was supposed to be up on the seventh floor making book marks out of cardboard and felt with all the other sick children. Because everyone on the ward was allowed to dress in their own clothes rather than hospital pyjamas, it was a small matter to simply shove your ID bracelet under your shirt sleeve and go wandering. And nobody said boo. But if a staff person from the ward caught you schmoozing in the lobby, as much as three weeks of privileges were forfeit. No television. No book marks or pool or video games in the Teen Lounge.

Of course, Mona had not just ridden up and down on the elevators and gone exploring the nether regions of the hospital like the rest of them typically did. She had left the building and disappeared into the city. She did not show up for dinner and there was a kerfuffle. Solomon was called and came to question Bridget. It was strange to see her in the evening.

"Did she say anything to you, Bridget?"

"Nope."

"Come on now, Bridget,"

"No, she really didn't. But look, she didn't take anything with her."

"Did she have any money hidden?"

"Ah, no, I don't think so," Bridget said. Because they weren't supposed to have any money hidden and both she and Mona did, in the ceiling tiles, along with Bridget's Mars bars and a bottle of Jim Beam that Stephen Cameron and Daniel Sutherland brought her one day when they were in town. But Bridget had been afraid to nip because of the smell. It seemed to her that the smell of liquor would simply rip through the aseptic corridors if she were to uncap it, bringing Gabby and the other staff on the run.

"Come on now, Bridget," Solomon persisted, well-trained and intuitive.

"Well, I don't know, maybe she did."

Solomon straightened up and looked at Gabby, who had begun glaring at Bridget upon hearing about the hidden money. Gabby liked to think that she ran a tight ship. "I suppose we'd better call the father," Solomon said to her.

Mona was back late the next afternoon, infuriating everybody. She had come back on her own and did not even have to be hauled from the streets by the police, who of course had been notified, and now had to be notified that they didn't need to look for her any more. She came in and threw a big bag of Hershey's Kisses on Bridget's bed.

"There ya go."

She sat down on the opposite bed and enthused to Bridget about what a wonderful city they were in and what a shame it was to be stuck in here all the time. She had gone to the punk bars and met millions of fucking awesome people. She had gotten toasted with the band and had sex with a guitarist who had hair down to his bum. She was still high, as a matter of fact. Then Gabby, jingling by to deliver someone's medication, happened to glance in Bridget's window and, too surprised to speak, proceeded to jangle frantically down the hall to tell Solomon that Mona was back. Bridget scurried to get her Hershey's Kisses into the ceiling.

"And I don't give a shit," Mona was going on, "what Mr. Asshole Motherfucker Wish-he-was-dead has to say about it. I'm moving here. I'm going to live here with Todd and them when I get out and live off my grandmother's inheritance (which was, Bridget gathered, grotesquely large and which Mona would come into in a few months, as soon as she turned eighteen). "This is the best place in the world," Mona said, "next to Florida." Solomon appeared with Gabby behind her and asked Mona to come into her office.

"Fuck you," Mona said, turning. She was glowing pink like an expectant mother. The sight of her made Bridget wince. There was something tragic about Mona's happiness. Like everything else she felt, her happiness, when it happened, was huge, infectious, could be felt in every corner as though Mona was a god and could make everybody feel what she was feeling. She was happy when the cafeteria sent up pizza or hot dogs for supper and she was happy at the thought of Bridget's mother and she was happy when the aerobics program came on television in the afternoons. And the problem with a happiness that large and unrestrained was the idea of it going away again, which was unbearable. Unbearable to Bridget, although Mona obviously never thought about that at the time of her happiness, otherwise she wouldn't be able to have it.

"I'm going to go to the *art college*," Mona said to Solomon. "And I'm going to take *pottery*," she proclaimed, standing up. She seemed about to make another even more significant proclamation to the powers that stood in front of her, but as an afterthought she turned to Bridget and said, "Did you know they have an art college here?"

"Your father has been very concerned," Solomon told her.

"My father sucks cocks."

"Language," said Gabby.

"He told me he would be flying in tonight," Solomon continued.

"Oh, cunt," said Mona, her face going from pink to black. "Tell him not to. Tell him I'm back now."

"I understand he's already on his way. He has some issues he wants to — "

"*Language*, Mona!" Gabby gasped, having only now recovered from "cunt."

Then Mona let Gabby have it. Like a backed-up sewer, her mouth exploded with filth. It was quite a moment. Solomon back-stepped daintily from the room to get one of the male staff on duty, Armand, to help them calm Mona down and the first thing Armand did was to tell Bridget — over Mona's hoarse shouts — to leave the room. Meanwhile, Gabby's training had kicked in and she was telling Mona that she could see that Mona was very upset right now and saying things she might not otherwise say under other circumstances.

"But it's my room," argued Bridget, for some reason.

"Other circumstances such as my grinding your face into a cheese grater, gash," Mona was saying.

"Bridget, please," said Solomon. So Bridget sidled past them all into the corridor, at the far end of which all the kids were assembled. They were standing very still, sniffing the air like prairie dogs.

"What's happening?"

"I dunno." Bridget went to watch TV.

The shouting seemed to go on forever, even after Mona was left to collect herself in the quiet room and there was no one there to shout at. It just went on and on, inarticulate, and when you left the TV room to go to the kitchen for dinner you had to pass by. It got louder and louder as you made your way down the corridor, resounding against the white walls, loudest when you got to the door. And then after you passed, it diminished, getting fainter. But you could still hear it all through dinner.

A little while after dinner, though, you couldn't any more. It was something else. It was the lyrics of Ike Turner, rendered in a wealthy, German-descended teenager's approximation of Tina.

> You're just a fool, you know you're in love,
> You got to face it to live in this world.
> You take the good along with the bad,
> Sometimes you're happy, and sometimes you're sad.
> You know you love him but you can't understand
> Why he treats you like he do
> When he's such a good man.

They had all followed Bridget into the TV room when she went. The kids on the ward were odd that way, they followed. They congregated, as on the day Bridget and Mona had crucified Byron in the kitchen. Everybody sensed where the thing of interest was and immediately materialized at that point. It was probably an instinct human beings naturally developed when thrust into situations of blinding ennui, like the ward. It was almost unnoticeable until you looked around and saw that the room was full. It was strange to look at the bunch of them. Disfunctionals. Egomaniacs like Byron who couldn't stand not to be seen and anorexics like Kelly who couldn't stand the opposite. Most of the boys on the ward looked like Byron, which Bridget thought was interesting. That is, they all looked terrible, precisely as if they belonged in the psychiatric ward of a hospital and not out among real people at all.

There was Shane, who was six feet tall, one foot of which had to be hair. He was pimply like Byron and stuttered so badly that there was no point in talking to him. And there was Jimmy, oversexed with a tongue too thick for his mouth and eyeballs going in opposite directions. There was a washer and dryer in the bathtub room, and if he ever heard the noise of one of the machines in operation Jimmy would always sneak in to press his genitals against it. Mona was constantly trying to catch him at it so she could tell the staff and see what they'd say.

In any event, what was interesting about all this was how the boys looked in contrast to the girls — the girls, that is, looked fine. The boys were freaks and the girls were just girls, the anorexics and bulimics drifting down the corridors like dustballs, inevitably delicate and otherworldly. Kelly, who had predictably burst into gutwrenching sobs at the sight of Bridget's angel food cake, was ethereal. Blonde and almost translucent, eighty-five pounds, and all the boys were in love with her. Byron followed her around, trying to tell her stories about how he used to be a vampire and smoothing back her flaxen hair and kissing her blue-veined forehead but, as far as Bridget knew, never going for the taco like he did with her and Mona. She reminded Bridget of those girls you read about in old fashioned novels, all white-skinned and swooning at a glance. Like Kelly, they never ate, could scarcely look at food, and their breathing always seemed laboured. Kelly walked around looking pained at everything. The sight of food caused her pain. Mona's loud laughter caused her pain. Byron's telling her how beautiful she was made her ache. Bridget's cake almost drove her round the bend.

To be fair, though, there was at least one girl on the ward who looked as if she belonged in the same category as the boys, an anti-Kelly, another anorexic named Maria about whom there was nothing otherworldly in the least because she was obviously so close to the physical reality of death. She had rotten teeth and hair like that on an old, abandoned doll. Maria had apparently been living on the ward for over four years and, like Kelly, she was only fifteen. There was no getting around the cliché that Maria resembled a Holocaust victim. She walked and talked in slow motion. Her bad teeth looked too big for her face. She was sickeningly shy and could not speak to anyone new on the ward until at least a month after their arrival. And when she spoke, it was so slow. She said to Bridget: "They told me that if I don't eat I'm never going to get out of here. They've been telling me that for years. And I don't care. I'm never going to eat." If you asked her why, she couldn't tell you, her brain had probably deteriorated so much that she couldn't remember. All Maria knew was that she was sticking to her guns, non-consumption was her raison d'être. Most of the time Maria was on bedrest with a needle in the back of her hand and a tube up her nose. She was the first person Bridget had ever met for whom she knew that death was imminent. And that was pretty much all there was to say about Maria, except that, shuffling down the corridor in her huge hospital pyjamas to use the shower room, Maria's shape was that of a big, elongated question mark.

There was something frightening about being in the same room with the lot of them, they were all so strange. You could say anything. It was not like being at school, where you were constantly on your guard *not* to seem weird. Here the strangeness was a given. It made Bridget tense because it was like vertigo. The temptation was to seize the opportunity to be weird, to revel in the fact that anything you said or did in front of these people was of no consequence. It was the fear of falling into madness, the easiest thing to do under the circumstances. The only thing that was, in fact, expected of you. Whenever they were all together, the air was full of that feeling because some of them had already succumbed to it, and sometimes — unless you were talking about a crying fit, but sometimes even then — it didn't look that bad. In conversation they seemed to circle each other, looking for cracks.

Bridget stretched out on the couch because she didn't want any of them sitting next to her. She didn't know what else to do, so she pretended that she was going to sleep.

"I know you're not sleeping, Miss Murphy," said Byron. Byron never used Bridget's first name.

"I'm trying to, so shut up," she replied. Mona's voice had travelled down the hall, around the corner, and into their ears. "Horse's twat!" it said.

"What happened?" Kelly asked hungrily. Everything about her was hungry.

"Mona came back, and she's pissed off that they called her father," Bridget answered with her eyes closed. She was ready to start snoring.

"Aha!" Byron said with much significance. Bridget opened her eyes to slits and saw him standing up with his arms folded, like he was about to make a speech. "Now she'll know!"

"Know what?" said Bridget, opening her eyes all the way.

"Not to mess with me."

"It doesn't have anything to do with you."

"Yes it does," he said, "because I put a hex on her. I told her I can do things. I told you both, and you laughed at me."

"Have you noticed that you're on a mental ward? Has it occurred to you that maybe it's ideas like these that have put you here?"

"I know exactly why I'm here," he said in his favourite, ominous way.

Bridget sat up. "This place is nuts."

Shane was sitting in a chair in the far corner twitching quietly to himself. He sputtered something at them.

"What, Shane?"

"They put drugs in the ventilation. They're doing experiments on us."

"They give us pills every day," said Bridget. "Why would they need to drug the air?"

"Oh my G-G-G-God," sputtered Shane, remembering the pills. Jimmy, who had taken out some Lego blocks and begun playing with them beside Shane's chair, started to laugh. Nobody noticed him. He was always laughing for no reason, as though he was remembering little jokes intermittently throughout the day. Sometimes he even laughed in his sleep, you could hear him down the hall.

Byron jumped up on the arm of the couch and stood there, balancing, trying to recapture everybody's gaze. "Listen to me!" he commanded, spreading his arms. It was the thing with Mona, Bridget knew. Mona was down the hall getting the attention of all the staff, and he didn't want that attention contaminating the patients as well. He was probably even jealous at the thought of her being put in the quiet room, which had up until now been almost exclusively his turf. It always had to be him. Thinking about Byron was the only thing that had gotten to Bridget in ages. And she hated that, because he would have loved it if he knew.

"Listen to me, look at me," she said, looking up at him. And Maria, this being one of the few days when she had ingested enough food to be allowed off bedrest for the afternoon, for some reason contributed in her dead voice, "I know!"

"You don't think I could put a hex on you, if I wanted to?" Byron said loudly, pimples alight.

"I think you already have," said Bridget.

"No, you don't even know what a hex is yet," he said, teetering back and forth on the arm of the couch.

"Yes, I do." said Bridget. "It's having to put up with a sad little nothing who's so insecure he has to make up stupid stories about himself that make him look even more pathetic . . ." She felt herself swinging into the same strange, detached mode of abuse that had overtaken her that time in the kitchen, and she felt the same mob mentality buzzing over the heads of everyone else in the room. Byron must've felt it too because he pounced on her, sort of. Not touching her, but jumping on to the chesterfield and then sort of hovering in the air above her with his arms raised over his head like the vampire he sometimes said he used to be.

"Haaaaah!" he yelled to try and make her stop talking. But Bridget kept on telling him what he was, even after Armand had come up behind Byron and plucked him off the couch. Even after Armand had dragged him down the hall, still all coiled up. Jimmy laughed the whole time and tossed his Lego blocks about like a two-year-old. Then Armand came back and told everyone to go find something to do. Bridget stood up, tingling as if she was coming down off a little high. What an evil thing boredom is, she thought then. She thought it had to be the most evil thing in the world. She used to think that was love.

It was remarkable, the swiftness with which Mona's father, Mr. Mona, descended and took her away. And even though nobody caught a glimpse of him, everybody seemed to know what had happened. He had bawled out Dr. Solomon, in the first place. Bawled her out! Apparently he was the kind of man who could bawl Dr. Solomon out. Furthermore, he kept calling the place a "facility," something Solomon would typically never have stood for. A hospital at worst, a healing environment preferably, but never something as impersonal and pre-Freud as a "facility." Nevertheless, Mr. Mona apparently called 'em as he saw 'em. What kind of facility was it, he wanted to know, that allowed its inmates ("inmates" must've smarted as well) to walk out the front door whenever they saw fit? This had to be the worst facility he'd ever put his daughter in.

We use the honour system here, Solomon must have replied with much indignation. Building up trust is crucial to the care-giver/care-recipient relationship. Or healer/healee relationship. Whatever jargon Solomon was making use of that day.

"What about ensuring that they aren't wandering the streets by themselves at night? Would you consider that crucial to the 'relationship,' Doctor?" Bridget knew that Mona's father was a lawyer. She lay on her bed fantasizing about a man who could bawl Solomon out, who could drop silently from the heavens with his talons extended and in the next instant ascend with them closed around a wriggling pink little Mona, the rest of the herd unperturbed and oblivious. Bridget did not miss her, although she did notice every day that she was gone. The ward became quieter. At night, no one snuck in to disturb her insomnia. Everything was simply less than it had been. The fluorescent lighting along the hallway seemed to have dimmed the slightest bit.

The lesson of all this, Bridget thought, was a good one. For every action there is an equal and opposite reaction, or something like that. Positive is always met by the negative. Or something. In any event. Inertia was the key.

The medication they were giving her seemed to agree on that point. They had switched it since the second incident of yelling at Byron. She felt even stupider than before and one time got on the elevator to go up to the Teen Lounge and couldn't remember how to work it. Byron would come into her room to read from a book about all the different hexes he could put on her if he wanted, and when he saw that she wasn't insulting him or telling him to leave or pretending that she was asleep, he assumed that she liked him and went for the taco again. So Bridget had to drag herself off the bed and lock herself in the bathroom until he left. It was no problem to disengage herself from Byron — he had the strength of paper.

In the bathroom she checked her underwear. She hadn't bled at all since the big blood-fest after The Birth. It had tapered off after a month or so and hadn't returned since. Which was nice, she supposed. So she wasn't bleeding and she wasn't shitting — that was nothing to complain about, especially since the initial discomfort of the latter had gone away as well. "Question of the day!" Gabby always gaily announced, poking her head into Bridget's room. It was her way of inquiring as to whether or not Bridget's bowels had moved. She always frowned and wagged her finger when Bridget said no, as if Bridget were deliberately holding back. "Epsom salts!" Bridget always told her, to which Gabby always replied: "You had your answer about that."

"What can you possibly have against Epsom salts, especially when you're giving me all these pills?" Bridget complained. "If you ask me, it's the pills that are doing it."

"No, Bridget, the medication doesn't do anything like that."

"What *does* it do? Is it a secret?"

She wasn't eating much either — except potatoes. The hospital meat was unnerving, but the potatoes were the opposite, always the same, two perfect, greyish semi-globes protruding from her plastic plate like a small, smooth set of tits. It was difficult to do culinary harm to potatoes. Gabby took note of this and made jokes about her being Irish. Bridget thought that there must be a million jocular remarks one could conceivably make about a Jewish Newfoundlander, but she kept this idea to herself, Gabby being one of those people who could dish it out but not take it.

Gabby and Solomon were the first Jewish people Bridget had ever met, and she wouldn't even have known this if the ever-worldly Albert hadn't made his point about Solomon, and if Gabby wasn't always bringing them Woody Allen movies on the weekends and explaining the religious references when she wasn't laughing herself sick. Bridget was only now beginning to realize that the rest of the world wasn't Catholic and felt foolish asking Gabby questions about what was going on in the films. Gabby always made vicious fun of her whenever Bridget thought she had witnessed something she could relate to.

"This could be my family," Bridget observed one time, "if they were a little more pissed off, and dumber."

"Oh, and one other thing, Bridget. No Christ," Gabby spat.

"No what?"

"Christ."

"Oh."

"Or funny little hats," Mona added, when Mona was there. Mona had hated the films and exercised the whole time they were on. Mona's favourite movie in the whole world was *A Clockwork Orange*, and Gabby wouldn't get it for them.

When Stephen Cameron and Daniel Sutherland came to see her, Bridget was eight feet in the air, at least. Byron had come in beforehand to discuss his latest spell and when Bridget pretended to go to sleep he amused himself by seeing how far he could crank up her hospital bed. Both of them were astounded by how high it had gone, right up to the ceiling. It weaved slightly, back and forth, causing Bridget to sit very still.

"What possible purpose could it serve like this?" Byron mused to himself before deciding it would be funny to go away and leave Bridget up there. So Bridget continued to read her book and waited for one of the staff to come along and get her down. She wasn't going to give Byron the satisfaction of hearing her yell for them. Instead, Stephen Cameron and Daniel Sutherland showed up, Stephen looking grave in his long black coat and Daniel all gangly as usual, like he would trip over the first step he took. She had not seen them for months. They were not really her friends, but Mark's friends, although Mark hadn't seen much of them either, ever since having got together to play "Sweet Home Alabama" over and over again with George Matheson.

Gravely Stephen cranked her bed back down and asked how she was doing once they were at eye level. Bridget said she was good. Daniel asked if he was allowed to smoke, and Bridget said she didn't think so. Daniel looked as if he felt guilty for having asked. Bridget asked what they were doing in town, and Stephen answered that Daniel was going to school up there now and Stephen had just come up to party for the weekend. Daniel added that Stephen had been puking all morning. Then Daniel laughed and Stephen twitched with irritation. Stephen, Bridget saw, was taking this all very seriously.

"I feel that I should have done something," Stephen said after a while.

And Bridget thought, with more lucidity than usual: You feel that I'm more interesting now that I've had a baby. And because I'm in a mental ward. I'm living the dream of Pink Floyd fans everywhere. I've tapped into the Great Sadness, and you want a piece of it. So that you can write songs, and poetry.

Bridget said, "What could you have done?"

"I don't know. I don't know. I could have talked to you guys. Maybe I can still help."

Silently, for no reason in particular, Daniel decided that this was the time to reach into his coat pocket for the pint of Jim Beam. He handed it to Bridget and Stephen blinked at him, not having expected it.

"It's been there since yesterday. I forgot I had it," Daniel explained to Stephen. They watched Bridget climb up onto a chair and shove the bottle into the ceiling. A Mars bar fell on her head. It only occurred to her later on that they could not have had any idea as to why she was keeping things in the ceiling. They wouldn't know about Gabby's thorough-going room raids. Nevertheless, they watched with silent deference as she retrieved the Mars bar and replaced it behind the tiles.

"There's nothing more to be done," Bridget said, throwing herself back down on the bed. "Thanks, though."

"I want you guys to be happy," Stephen stressed. *You guys* set off a vague sort of alarm in her head. "Mark has really had a hard time . . ."

"I don't want to hear about Mark," Bridget said. What she had almost said was, I don't care about Mark.

"I think you guys need to talk."

"We don't need to talk." But she saw with hopelessness that Stephen was never going to believe this. Stephen was never going to believe that a thing had happened and was over. That a thing could be so entirely annihilating that the things responsible for it happening in the first place were not there any more. Not even in ruins, but gone. So gone that they couldn't even be remembered, let alone remembered fondly or sadly.

Stephen thought that she wasn't sincere. He couldn't conceive of her saying something like that and meaning it. That was why he was out there, and she was in here.

"It really hurt him, you taking up with that old guy," Stephen went on. He still thought that she would want to hear about things like what had hurt him and what hadn't. She couldn't even imagine anybody being hurt by anything. And then she began to laugh, realizing that by "that old guy" Stephen meant Alan Voorland. Poor Alan. Everyone thought he was older than he was because of his beard and his little pot belly. Stephen watched her laugh, arranging his face to look stricken. Daniel, meanwhile, seemed to writhe in his seat on the opposite bed. Bridget thought he was aware that this visit wasn't fair. Bridget wished it was just Daniel who had come. Daniel would have handed her the Jim Beam and left, decently.

"He's not that old," Bridget said at last. "He's only twenty-five."

"Well, that's not really the point."

"Christ Almighty, Stephen, I can't believe you've come here to tell me what a bad person I am."

Stephen was startled. It might have occurred to Stephen that he'd been listening to only one side of the story for a very long time. He worked at Home Hardware full time now with Mark. Stephen wanted to take a couple of years off before university and was planning on going to Europe with his Home Hardware earnings. Bridget could picture the two of them, stocking shelves side by side. The words bitch, cunt, and selfish drifting up from the conversation every once in a while. Stephen nodding sympathetically.

"I haven't," said Stephen, pained. "I want to help you guys."

"Then quit saying 'you guys.'"

"When are you coming home, anyway?"

"Home?"

"Yeah."

"I don't know."

"Christmas?"

"I don't know."

"Well, they must be letting you come home for Christmas," he insisted.

"I suppose so," said Bridget.

"You don't know? It's just around the corner. Only twenty shopping days left."

"Holy shit," marvelled Bridget, who hadn't noticed. Who had scarcely noticed the wind pulling the leaves off the trees or the grass gone yellow or the snow-dust filling in the cracks in the sidewalks outside. And there began for Bridget a lifelong personal tradition of dread every year in anticipation of Christmas. Because Christmas would always mean going home and never knowing who you were going to run into.

CHAPTER 7

Her father was a craftsman. Once he had worked for the government, had practically run the town at one point, but residents soon became appalled at the kind of upheaval he was constantly trying to achieve. He had wanted to build a senior citizens' home, for one thing. He had wanted Causeway Days — the spring festival — to attract more tourists, to entail more than a five-float parade down the main street, two of which were always furnished by the mill, three of which were no more than locals in toilet paper-decorated pickups with signs on the front reading stuff like: "JimmyArchie's Lumber" or "Come to MacIntyre's Big Stop. Two for 99 on O Henrys." Bridget's father had also wanted some kind of musical event other than the traditional bagpipe contest that led him to refer to the festival as "Cat Killing Days" during an interview at the local radio station. Many residents had been offended. They were proud of the bagpiping contest. It was one of the many things that made the community unique. They found Mr. Murphy to be overbearing and unduly aggressive. One day her father came home late from a meeting and announced, "Piss on 'em. They can play the bagpipes till their foolish lungs implode. I hope they all go as deaf as me arse." And he went downstairs to work on his craft.

Woodworking was his craft. He called it that, but it was really more like art. Nobody dared suggest this to him. Once, a TV station out of Halifax had called him up to be on some program about Maritime folk art. "I'm no dope-smoking hairy-faced fruit," was

73

what he said. "Unlike you and yours." Television was television to her father — Halifax no different from Los Angeles. "Ar-teests," he'd spit, whenever the subject came to mind, making flitting gestures with his short yellow fingers. "Arse-tits is more like it."

So her father was a craftsman of wood. He drove off into the hills every Sunday to pick choice pieces. He especially liked the trees that had some disease which made the wood bulge out monstrously in places, as if gourds had become stuck in the trunks somehow. Her father liked to take the diseased trunks home and carve all sorts of faces into the bulges. If there were a lot of bulges, the effect was very much like a totem pole — caricatures of bulbous-nosed hobos and sailors replacing those of owls and wolves and ravens. Bulbous-nosed, heavy-lidded men's faces were one of her father's specialties. At other times he would come home with what appeared to be an average piece of wood, spend a few hours sanding and varnishing it, and then present it to the family — a smooth, polished piece of wood.

"Whaddya think of that?"

"It's really nice!"

"You see what it is?"

"Um. A fish?"

"It's a wolf's head. See, there's its snout. By God, nature does the work, I just bring it to the fore."

Mr. Murphy also delighted in any chunk of wood that bore a passing resemblance to parts of the human anatomy. He stole a pair of his wife's shoes once to put on a branch uncannily like a bum and a pair of legs — right down to having little protrusions where the feet would be. This was where he hung the shoes. Bridget's mother got mad because they were good shoes, but he wouldn't let her replace them with a pair of old slippers or anything. He referred to the artifact, for some reason, as Mrs. MacGillicutty, and pretty soon, after he had returned gleeful from the woods one day with what he said was a husband for Mrs. MacGillicutty, Bridget's mother wouldn't go down to his shop any more.

The shop did a fairly good business because he made cabinets as well and because he over-priced his art work outrageously for the tourists. He had also acquired a reputation for being a character, and local people were always stopping by to see what he'd do. They found his insults endearing, but if ever they loitered too long, he'd bark, "If you're not buying, you're leaving," in a deliberately less charming kind of way, in such a way as to make them fear they had offended him somehow. In such a way as to prompt them to buy, perhaps, one of his twenty-five-dollar golf balls. For those, he peeled away half of the ball's pitted skin and then carved goofy faces into the hard rubber beneath. Everyone thought this was ingenious.

What a lot of people really came for, though, were Bridget's father's decoys. His decoys were simply beautiful, more beautiful than any actual duck. They were completely smooth and flawless — he did not bother with feathers of any other realistic detail that might disturb the decoy's linearity. The result was a perfect, liquid platonic ideal. Perfect duckness. He stained — never painted — and then varnished them. The wood was what mattered. The acknowledgement and refinement of the wood rather than any attempt to deny it was what made the carvings very nearly sublime. People came from far and wide to purchase one of Bridget's father's ducks. They were all exactly the same.

The most recent news from home was that her father had started bringing Rollie down to the basement with him, and now Rollie was an artist, a craftsman, too.

Rollie's school had been shut down. Rollie used to go to a special school every day where he would make bread with other adults like himself. The bread was very good, and Bridget's mother bought loaves of it every week. It spoiled the family for the store-bought kind, and on weekends, if they ever ran out, Gerard would sometimes go on rampages, rummaging through the deep freeze in hopes of finding a forgotten loaf, hollering, "Where's the retardo bread?"

Rollie loved going to school, and if Bridget's parents wanted to punish him for not going to bed when they told him to, or taking a piss out of doors, or pulling his shorts up over his belt and ripping them, then they wouldn't let him go. It was a very effective punishment, and they were relieved to finally have discovered some kind of leverage to use against him. It was widely acknowledged within the family that Peter Joseph Pat and Margaret P. had spoiled Rollie most of his life, cutting his meat and pouring his tea and putting his mittens on for him and not letting him do anything on his own, and so when it came time for Rollie to live under Bridget's father's rule, Rollie knew how to be quite stubborn. Bridget's father didn't know any way to make him do anything except for cursing at him and giving him the occasional shove up the stairs. It was still a little difficult with Margaret P. around. Sometimes Rollie would stumble into her room in tears and Margaret P. would bang on the wall with her bedpan, wanting to know what had been done to him.

"Jesus Murphy, Ma, I was just trying to get him to take off his own goddamn shoes!"

"Well, he can't take off his shoes, you know, he's never taken off his shoes."

"He's never *had* to take off his own shoes, for the love of God!"

Bridget's father saw that changes had to be made, and so he sent Rollie to the special school as soon as it opened up. Rollie surprised everybody by loving it. He had even managed to acquire something like a girlfriend, a woman named Emma, overweight and always smiling. Every night before going to bed Rollie would ask Bridget's father, "Who's going to wake him up for school see Emma?" and her father would revel in his new-found power.

"Well, now, I don't know if any one *should* wake you up for school, not coming in for supper when Joan calls you."

"He'll come in for supper."

"You will, eh? You're not going to do that again, walking around in circles going no, no, no, like a Jesus lunatic?"

"No, he's not."

"You're going to come in next time, then, are you?"

"No he's not, no he's not," Rollie would say rapidly, putting his hands over his ears.

"Well, are you going to come in next time or aren't you?"

"He's going to come in next time."

"All right then. Go on up to bed."

"Who's going to wake him up for school, Raw-hurt?"

"Robert will wake him up for school."

But now, due to lack of resources, Rollie's school was shut down. It was a trying time for everyone. Bridget's father didn't know what was to be done with Rollie during the day. He sat in his chair with the television on and would complain, "When's Rollie going to school see Emma?" every time Bridget's mother or father went by. This, along with his queries about Bridget's whereabouts, was combining to drive the two of them up the wall. So one day Bridget's father announced: "Shit on this. You come on downstairs with me, sir. We'll get you going at something."

This was how Rollie became an artist. Not just an artist, but, according to Bridget's father, a religious artist, the best and only kind of artist to be. Her father had stuck a piece of wood into Rollie's hand and let him go at it with the sander. So Rollie stood there, humming to himself and sanding and sanding the wood until Bridget's father took it away from him and held it up to the light. There and then he declared the overly sanded block of wood to be uncannily, one might even say miraculously, representative of the Virgin holding the baby Jesus. He ran to show it to Bridget's mother and asked if she agreed, and Bridget's mother said that she supposed so, and so he hurried back down to the basement to varnish the new work and put it on display, stopping only to hand Rollie another piece of wood to get started on.

According to Bridget's mother, Rollie was becoming famous. Her father had a whole display of his religious carvings lined up on the shelf above the golf balls. Little cards in front of each announced what the wooden blobs were supposed to represent, from "Jesus Heals the Sick" to "Saint Paul on the Road to Damascus." Some people who came into the shop seemed initially dubious about the carvings until Mr. Murphy explained who had done them. He dar-

ingly set them at the same price as his carved golf-balls, a great favourite among locals and tourists alike, and in a flash of inspired
business savvy put up a bigger sign above them all which read:

Religious Wooden Statues.
Done by Retarded Man.
Twenty-five dollars a piece.

And now they were her father's number-one seller. Even more
than the ducks. They were especially popular with Christmas on its
way. Bridget's father, in anticipation of the season, glued sprigs of
plastic holly to the occasional piece.

Bridget was to come home to them for the holiday, just as Stephen
Cameron had supposed, and Dr. Solomon had been happy to inform her that she didn't think there was any need for her to come
back as an in-patient.

"As an outpatient, then?" Bridget asked, feeling, to her surprise,
something like panic.

"Do you feel you'd like to keep seeing someone on a semi-regular
basis? Yes, I would agree with that. I'm afraid the trips into town
would be costly for your parents, though. Maybe we could come to
an arrangement with Inverness . . ."

"I could go to school up here," said Bridget, surprising herself
again. "I could get a loan to go to the art college."

"I had no idea you were interested in studying art!"

"I could take pottery," said Bridget.

So Solomon informed Bridget's parents, with considerable pleasure she said, that Bridget had expressed an interest in going to school
in the city and attending the art college. Bridget lay on her bed imagining how her father must have responded to this. He would never
say anything to her. He never said anything to her, but he would
certainly be saying something. Probably to her mother. Unfortunately for her mother, Bridget's father said everything he didn't say
to Bridget to Joan. He spoke through her. Bridget's mother said she
was like the Virgin Mary that way. And if Gerard got anything from

his father, a notion that would make the former squirm, it was Raw-hurt's contempt for the arts. Gerard called up a few days later to make arrangements for the drive home and told Bridget that if she ended up getting thousands of government dollars to learn how to make bowls he would kill himself. Gerard himself was studying to be an engineer, like Alan Voorland.

"Fuck it," opined Alan Voorland to her over the phone. "Make bowls. Just don't go back there if you can help it."

"I can't help it. I have to go back for Christmas."

"Can't you fake a massive psychotic episode or something?"

Bridget thought about it. Not enough energy.

"When are you coming back?" Alan wanted to know.

"The fifteenth. When are you leaving?"

"The twelfth," said Alan Voorland. "Fucking hell. I want to see you before I go."

"Come up before you go."

"Oh, God, I can't, I've barely got enough time to wrap everything up as it is. Besides, they'd never let me take you out overnight. Would they?"

"It doesn't need to be overnight."

"You have no idea," said Alan.

"No, I don't," she said. "Anyway, you'll have your girlfriend soon for all that stuff."

"Christ, you really do have no idea."

You'd think that would make a difference to you, Bridget thought. But she laughed and said, "Quite the cad."

"Quite the cad. Please don't remind me what a cad I am."

They breathed into the phone at each other for a couple of moments.

"Don't come back here," he said for the hundredth time.

"Why, what's been going on?"

"Nothing. Nothing. Dead. I can't wait to get out."

"Well I have to go back for Christmas."

"Yeah, but I can't see you leaving again. Come up with me."

"To Guelph?" She was surprised that he would ask her this a second time.

"Yeah. There's a university."

"But do they teach pottery, that's the question. Because I can't go anywhere where they don't have pottery."

So Alan Voorland was to disappear into central Ontario along with Mona. She had no expectation of seeing either of them again, but this was probably because she never thought about the future at all. A little while after Mona had gone, Bridget heard from her, in a manner of speaking. Bridget had been feeling around behind the ceiling tiles for her half-empty bag of Hershey's Kisses and found one of Mona's books instead. Mona liked fantasy novels, the kind that described a lot of buxom, sword-wielding amazon women, with whom she could identify, partaking in equal quantities of sex and violence. This one was called *Women of the Trinity*, which Bridget thought sounded blasphemous. The book bulged with scraps of paper that Mona must have been using to mark the pages. There was also writing on a couple of them, along with some notes she had made in the margins, most of which declared simply, "ME!!!" But one of the loose scraps read:

> *Chewing on carrion Chewing on carrion*
> *existing exciting eternal in*
> *Glorious liquid shit*
> *But most of all*
> *Chewing on carrion and sucking everything out*

And another scrap read: IF I COULD GROW MY HAIR AS LONG AS RAPUNZEL THE FUNNIEST FUCKING THING IN THE WORLD WOULD BE TO ASK SOME ONE TO CLIMB UP IT AND THEN CUT IT ALL OFF BEFORE HE GOT THERE.

Bridget didn't know if the book constituted the only kind of diary Mona's attention span would allow or else some kind of cryptic message to herself. This seemed possible, in spite of the fact that there were no direct references to her, because even when the two of them were having a conversation Mona rarely made any direct reference to Bridget. Mona's eternal point of reference had been herself. Another reason Bridget suspected that Mona may have left the book for her was that two of her tarot cards were jammed together between the pages, facing one another. And one was Mona's own, the one with the lady and the lion on it and the other one was the queen of swords. The only thing was that Mona had said Bridget was the page of swords, not the queen, so she wasn't sure. Either way, she thought she liked the queen of swords better. She liked how she just sat there, unsmiling and plain in contrast to the other queens Mona had showed her. Holding a sword and pointing at it.

The disfunctionals began acting oddly towards her once they found out that Bridget was leaving. Byron kept saying, "You think you're leaving? You're not leaving."

"Solomon says I'm leaving."

"You're not leaving."

They started coming to her, which was bizarre. One would come into her room and sit on the opposite bed and attempt to make innocuous conversation. And soon another one would notice the first one in there with Bridget and decide to join them. And pretty soon the ward telepathy took over, and Bridget found herself holding a kind of aseptic court under the fluorescent lighting, interrupted only by Gabby poking her happy head in to ask the question of the day. Gabby was overjoyed to see them all in one place, not having to track them down. She was also, perhaps, curious to see them finally turning themselves into a community of sorts, considering that the only thing everybody on the ward had in common was their singularity. It was what had put them there, this state of egregiousness. And just because they were presently in a place where everyone else was egregious, too, didn't mean they were about to give it up, this status. Up until now they had obliviously passed one another in the corridors like ghosts in the Tower of London. Anne Boleyn shuffling past a treacherous soldier, head tucked under her arm, six fingers cradling the blueish face. Each from their own particular period in history, so neither aware of the other's presence.

In her last couple of weeks on the ward, Bridget found out more about the people she was living with than she had over the space of four months. Why was this? She was never interested before, but she also wasn't interested now. It had to be because of them, because of their becoming interested in Bridget's knowing about them. It was as if she were about to depart from some isolated colony — they wanted her to take all their messages to the outside world.

Byron was the only one whose messages Bridget was used to hearing, but now he became positively frenzied to explain himself to her. Bridget would languish on her bed making fun of him, entertaining the court, but Byron wouldn't stop.

"All you guys want to go home. You want to get out of here. You can't wait to get out of here. You don't know anything. You don't deserve to be in here if you want to get out."

"That makes tremendous sense."

"I'm glad I'm here. I hope they keep me here for the next twenty years."

"As do, I'm sure, all of us who are going to be on the outside" (laughter from the court).

"I'd rather be here than at home any day," Byron continued helplessly.

Byron's problem was, he said, that his parents were stupid. His parents didn't even come close to approaching his own intellectual capacity. He spoke of their "staggering stupidity" with considerable loathing. Bridget had seen them once and couldn't deny it. Had walked in on them in the TV room where they were visiting with Byron. They were both smoking and had their feet up on the coffee table as though it were their own living room, oblivious to the cartoon characters painted on the windows and the stack of board games and ice cream bucket full of Lego blocks sitting in the corner. They were both overweight, dressed with embarrassing care in unfortunately patterned clothing. His mother had a terrible, barking voice which Byron twitched at. She called him Ronnie.

"Gonna introduce us to yer friend, Ronnie? Hah?"

"Bridget, this is my parents."

"Whadda you in for, dear? She looks fine to me."

Bridget said, "Thank you," backing out into the hall.

It was true, they were nothing like Byron at all.

"I think I'm adopted," Byron confided to the court. "They won't tell me if I am or not. But I know I am. I even think I know who my real parents are." He looked around at them, supposing his pause was building an unbearable suspense.

"Well, the suspense is unbearable," Bridget commented.

"You'll never know what it's like to be adopted!"

"I'm adopted, for Christ's sake," she said.

Byron had been sitting cross-legged on the opposite bed, face resting in hands, elbows resting on thighs. Throughout the dialogue he had been rocking back and forth, staring at the vomit-green woollen hospital blanket. Now he rocked to a slow stop and looked up at Bridget.

"You are?"

"Yes."

"Why didn't you tell me before?"

"Because, for those of us who really are adopted and aren't just fantasizing about it as a way of distancing themselves from their stupid parentage, it's not a big deal."

Kelly asked, "Don't you want to know about your real parents?" and Byron gave her a dirty look, as he had accepted Bridget's answer and was ready to swing back into the story of himself.

Bridget was about to say, "Yeah, but they let you find out when you're twenty-one," because this is what she had always planned to do. Her parents had been the ideal adoptive couple. They were fashionable in the spring of 1970; in fact, they were probably the seventies equivalent of Yuppies, and adoption was a fashionable alternative to the infertile pre-Yuppie couple in those days. Or so Bridget had gathered. Her parents, when they had actually been making money and the world was very much their oyster, thought there was no other bureaucracy of such humane beauty as the modern legal adoption system: The government would take the children of poor, foolish girls and give them to the stable and well-to-do. The dual plagues of abortion and infertility done away with in one magnanimous legal swoop. The process was only marred, for Bridget's mother and father, by the considerable time it took.

Her parents took pains never to hide this from Bridget or Gerard, a few years earlier. They read them stories with titles like "The Chosen Child," which glorified the process by which the two of them had actually been "picked" out of, presumably, a whole nursery full of babies, waiting like puppies behind a pet store window. The book dictated that this should make children like Bridget and Gerard feel special, but actually such stories turned out to be counterproductive because, knowing nothing of the birds and the bees at such an age, Bridget and Gerard both naturally assumed that all babies were selected by their parents in this way.

Pretty soon, though, the two of them figured things out. And Bridget's parents lost no time in making it known that she and Gerard would be perfectly free to find out all they could about their "birth" parents once they turned twenty-one. So this was what Bridget had always thought she would do. Gerard was twenty-one now but had never cared about any of that stuff, he said. And Bridget, thinking about it, found that it wasn't all that interesting to herself any more, either.

"No — what difference does it make?" Bridget answered Kelly.

"That's funny, 'cause I always thought you looked like your mother," Kelly mused. This was laughable. The warped perception of the disfunctional. Bridget's mother was five foot two and had no body to speak of. Her slight figure practically shouted its infertility to the world.

Bridget smirked. "Are you kidding?"

"No, I mean around the face, kinda," persisted Kelly.

Bridget had been listening to Kelly more and more. She said odd, sometimes interesting things which Bridget never expected. She had dismissed Kelly at first because she was so blonde and ethereal and because she was anorexic. It all seemed to fit together, Bridget having always assumed that anorexics were just girls wanting to get on the cover of *Glamour*.

But everything made Kelly ache, that was why. Everything caused her pain. She was constantly trying to escape sensation. Food, she said, made her sick. It was gross, and she resented the necessity of it. "Do you know," she said, "if I wanted to go off and wander around in the desert, I couldn't do it? Because I would have to eat. I would have to be eating all the time. It would get in the way of everything."

"You could just bring a bunch of food."

"No, that's not the point. I couldn't just go there, I couldn't just up and go there. It would ruin everything."

"You would have to sleep anyway."

"Sleeping's fine. I don't mind sleeping. It's no problem to fall asleep."

It is for me, thought Bridget. Although she knew that she must be sleeping some. She couldn't be staying awake all night, every night, or else she wouldn't be able to function. Sometime between six and nine, the least lucid time of her so-called sleep period, the time that stood out in her memory with the least clarity, she had to be dozing.

Sometimes Kelly and Maria would come to see Bridget together. They had formed an alliance of sorts in their mutual antagonism towards consumption. Sometimes they would share with Bridget cryptic anorexic observances.

"Did you notice that, no matter how fat you get, your shoes always stay the same size? You can wear the shoes of someone ten times skinnier than you, but that's it. You can't wear her shirt or her pants."

"Extremities," agreed Maria in her utterly slow delivery. "Head . . . hands . . . and . . . feet. They don't get fat."

"No, that's right, they don't."

Kelly was being put on bedrest more and more, almost as often as Maria. The ward's emphasis on routine, on the rigorous scheduling of every meal and activity, worked against them where the anorexics were concerned. Kelly and Maria loved routine. They loved the idea of pre-decided meals being sent up at specific times throughout the day. It helped them to consolidate their own schedules. Wednesday: breakfast, nine thirty a.m. Two slices whole wheat toast, cereal, orange juice. Eat one half slice of one of the pieces of toast, no butter. Take one sip of orange juice to keep the staff happy. Push cereal around with spoon. Twelve thirty p.m., lunch. Apple, tuna salad sandwich, carton of milk, fruit cocktail. Eat one half of the apple, or the whole thing if it's small. Ask for a glass of water.

The staff had figured this out, and so that was where bedrest came in. Bedrest was a luxury longed for by most of the other residents because you got to stay in bed all day and could eat whatever you wanted, whenever you wanted. All you had to do was ask for something and it was brought up to you from the kitchen no matter what time of the day. And you were certainly not expected to partake in any of the idiotic activities devised by the staff, like painting cartoon characters, Garfield, Archie and the Gang, on the windows. Or playing marathon Monopoly. It was a ward for children, the whole hospital was for children, but most of the people on the psychiatric ward, with only a couple of exceptions, were in their teens. Bridget didn't think it was like that in any of the other wards. Teenagers with real illnesses were admitted into the adult hospital down the street, where Bridget had come from. So in a way she had bureaucratically gone from adult status, in giving birth, to that of a child, in being depressed. It was all as arbitrary as the days were long.

CHAPTER 8

They used to do things that, if she described them to anyone, would sound romantic. So perhaps it was no wonder, Mark being pissed once he got wind of it. And with *that old guy*. How slutty. She imagined them, he and George and Chantal, huddled in the basement shit-box, Pink Floyd's "Mettle" low and psychotic in the background, speculating about the relationship, its no-doubt sordidness. And *with child*, Mark's, God. Had she no shame? In the end, Bridget was sure they had it figured that she had been taking money from poor old Alan Voorland.

They would go for walks on the beach at night, for example. Drive all the way out to Port Hood just for the pleasure of the warm June air and the water sounds and the moon, the June moon. And Alan would often put his arm around her. So yes, they must have looked like a romantic couple. Anyone would have thought so. Any of the girls from school. Heidi, for example, would have shrieked in her high-school-girl way, "Omigo-odd!" delighted and scandalized. Sometimes it even seemed as though Alan was caving in to it. And he could sense when she was sensing that, and would squeeze her a little harder to show it wasn't true, just good clean affection for good old Bridget Murphy.

"Don't worry, I'm not falling in love with you."

"Good."

"Because I know that's the last thing you'd want."

"That's right."

"What would you do if I did, though?"

"I dunno."

"You'd probably pull away from me, wouldn't you?"

"Probably."

"Why?"

Disgust, she thought.

"You're in no position to start a new relationship," Alan answered for her.

"That's right, I'm in no position."

They would go back up to Creignish Mountain with beer and wine, which Bridget was able to stomach again, and Alan would continue to ask questions of her. She thought it was remarkable that he still wanted to know things about her. She scarcely asked him anything about himself, and that hadn't fazed him either. He kept telling and he kept asking, he was not deterred. This was what she liked about Alan and would always like about him. He was a rigorous friend. It was possible to be utterly listless around him and yet have the friendship remain intact. He would hold up both sides of it if need be.

This *was* friendship, she told herself, and because it was the one good thing left, she tried not to admit to herself that it could be anything else, like infatuation. The allure of a quiet, tortured, passive teenager. Earlier in the friendship, a neon sign would flash every once in a while when Alan was being particularly solicitous. The sign said: EVERY MALE OVER TWENTY YEARS OF AGE WANTS TO PORK A SEVENTEEN YEAR OLD, STUPID-ARSE.

So Bridget had cynically thought that as soon as any pawing commenced, which it had right there on Creignish Mountain, she would let the fantasy play itself out. And now that it had, Alan, impressively, was still there and hadn't touched her since. Maybe it was guilt, knowing she hadn't asked for it or particularly needed it at that point in time. Or maybe it was as simple as the fact that touching Bridget had probably been a lot like the feel of meat before it goes into the pan.

Yet when Bridget talked to him on the phone from the hospital, he wanted to take her out overnight. He had seemed very intent on this. So perhaps Alan thought that things were different, now, that maybe her passionlessness, the thing he supposed was responsible for the deadness of her flesh, had expelled itself since August. He might have thought that. They had not seen each other since early July. But now he would never know either way — because Alan, after all, had gone home.

On Creignish Mountain, they would lean back in the bucket seats of Alan's Escort and look at the stars. Another romantic venture, if you chose to view it that way. Except that Bridget felt nothing. Was feeling less and less every day. She looked at the stars and saw them for what they were.

"Do you fantasize?" he asked.

"Why do you ask me that?"

"Because you don't seem like you fantasize, but then I think, *everybody* fantasizes."

"You mean sexually?"

"Whatever."

"No."

"Not at all?"

"Well, do you mean about sex or what?"

"Well, I was hoping to hear about sex."

"Then, no."

"Well, do you fantasize at all?"

"I dunno."

"Freud would say all fantasies are about sex."

"Would he?"

"I don't know, actually. I imagine he would."

Bridget thought back to when she was thirteen or so. She used to fantasize the way Mona probably fantasized, although she didn't know who Mona was yet, sitting there with Alan on the mountain. She fantasized about mythical times, riding a horse, carrying a sword and a big book of spells. Magic powers. Doing battle against the forces of evil, hair going everywhere. She had never played Dungeons and Dragons, but probably some kind of generational osmosis had taken place in this respect since she knew of so many others who did. Mark had told her of all-night sessions in Daniel Sutherland's candlelit basement, Led Zepplin on the stereo. But there was no way she could be bothered telling Alan any of this. It was, she suspected, the adolescent equivalent of being six years old and wanting to be a princess when you grew up.

"You really don't have sexual fantasies?"

"Really, no."

"Freud would say you're repressed."

"He probably would."

"So what do you fantasize about?"

It wasn't so much a fantasy, as . . . a thing. A thing that she did now. The stars reminded her of it. A few months ago, she remembered lying on her bed, sweating, systematically punching herself in the stomach. Thinking it would make her feel better, but it didn't, it didn't even have the gratification of pain. It seemed as if her arm was too close to her body to really build up any force, so the punches were actually no more than ineffectual flails at herself. Her body was designed, she realized, not to be able to hurt itself in this way. Her body thwarted her at every turn. Always. So eventually she had closed her eyes and tried not to think about it. And in trying not to think about it, she began to do this thing. And it had worked, to a point.

"I think about," she said to Alan, "space."

"Space? Like room?"

"Outer space."

"Good," he approved. "Captain Kirk?"

"No, no."

"*Star Wars*?"

"No, not space ships and all that."

"Then what?"

"Just being in space."

"And what else?"

"Stars."

"Planets?"

"No — stars, burning gases, far away."

"What else?"

"That's it."

Alan was quiet for a couple of moments, formulating. "You, in space . . ."

"Yeah."

" . . . with stars far away."

"Yes."

"You, in space, with stars far away. Burning gases. That's your fantasy, that gets you off."

"I didn't say it got me off, you said it didn't matter if it got me off."

"Obviously I didn't mean it."

The other thing about that particular evening was that around nine Alan drove her back to the apartment to listen to more Bessie Smith and hear some character sketches he had written about a couple of the guys at the mill whose personalities, he said, he "delighted in." Bridget reminded him that she had to be home by eleven because her parents thought she was working at one of the concerts. This caused Alan to shudder for a moment, holding the door of the building open for her.

"Parents. Eleven. Sneaking around on your parents, oh my God. Keep reminding me to keep my hands off your boobs."

And as fate would dictate, Chantal and George were just then coming up the steps from the basement shit-box. Since Alan had the door open anyway, and being the most instinctively courteous of men, it was only natural that he continue to hold it open for the two of them. Both George and Chantal's eyes were at half-mast, and the smell that typically overpowered the apartment — hash — hung thickly around them. Bridget knew precisely where they were going, having staggered along with them to get chips and dip and ice cream at MacIssac's Variety countless times in the past.

It was sheer niceness on the part of God not to have included Mark in the encounter. Nonetheless, there would be repercussions. Oh yes. She could already see them in the dark little eyes. Chantal, eternally spoiling for a fight, a new enemy. There were so many people like that. Mark, in fact, was like that. Her father was like that. Chantal's haze had lifted and Bridget watched her face go vulpine with anticipation. Bridget hadn't been to the shit-box in a month and had no doubt of her current status. Everybody knew that the girl wasn't supposed to dump the guy after getting pregnant. And now the righteous indignation emanating from the shit-box would be thicker than the waftings of hash and Hermit.

"How's she going?" chirped Alan, stupidly imitating the local idiom. George growled something in response. He growled everything, George, thinking it made him sexy to women, threatening to men. George was what her father would call a jeezless punk, with Harley Davidson pins puncturing the lapels of his leather jacket, and the hair — short in front, long in back. And of course he played guitar. The growl he gave Alan seemed to reinforce all of this as he shuffled through the door. Chantal only smiled, her cheekbones floating above her head. Bridget had a brief vision of staggering around the girl's bathroom with her hands to her throat, blood spurting between her fingers.

Funniest was the thing Alan said once they were gone, having no idea about anything: "I see even the Maritimes has white trash,"

You have more or less just pissed on my flag, she might have said to him then.

The Christmas season was terrible for everyone. Hospitals and sick children and Christmas were a gutwrenching combination, especially up in the Teen Lounge, where bruise-eyed thirteen-year-olds sat with their metal IV skeletons behind them, cutting holes into folded pieces of white paper for snowflake decorations. Others cut felt with pinking shears, gluing the shapes together to make bells, candles and holly. Once these were finished, the craft lady would string a piece of gold thread through the top because they were to be sold at the Christmas Craft Fair, all proceeds going to the Hospital for Sick Children, as tree ornaments.

Bridget was there too. She and the rest of them from the ward were being forced up daily to create their own individual masterpieces. Byron complained about it. He said it was hideous and "Dickensian" to force children who uniformly wanted to lie down and die into the lounge to listen to Burl Ives and toil on a felt-and-glitter production line. Gabby told him that a lot of the children found doing crafts therapeutic.

"What about those of us who don't find it therapeutic but a sadistic torment?"

"Some people don't know something will be therapeutic until they try it," Gabby soothed, shooing the herd into the elevator.

If Bridget got any pleasure from seeing Byron grimly hacking a swastika out of green felt to the tune of "Holly Jolly Christmas," it was only if she looked at him alone and none of the others sitting in a row at the long table. The sight of them made her think that he was right. Dying children shouldn't be expected to make Christmas ornaments out of felt. People would buy them at the craft sale and put them on their trees: Look! An actual dying child made this manger. We understand it was cystic fibrosis. And here's our leukemia candycane. And we got this wreath from the Indian reserve.

There was no denying that some of them probably did enjoy the diversion or were at least being diverted by it. One translucent fourteen-year-old girl, who Bridget, with her new-found expertise, at first would have diagnosed as anorexic but later learned had full blown AIDS, had a particular flair for the decorations. She would even twist the felt in elaborate ways to give the finished product a three-dimensional effect, and the craft lady would always hold her latest creations up to inspire everyone at the table and talk about the new dialysis machine or surgical laser it would help the hospital purchase. The girl would sneeze, picking up another wad of felt and eating some of the glue off her fingers.

Bridget was another of the craft lady's stars. Sick of the felt and glitter, she had been looking through some of the lady's craft books and come across what looked like a fairly easy method of making lovely, ornate snowflakes simply by curling strips of white paper and gluing them together. But she soon found out that it wasn't easy to do at all. It was extremely intricate work, and it took Bridget four days of her Teen Lounge time to complete the first one, which by all accounts was a masterpiece. The craft lady exhorted her to come up with at least five more before the sale, so Bridget began taking her work downstairs to the ward with her. The snowflakes required tremendous concentration. Bridget worked on them every spare moment, which in her present mode of existence meant practically all the time. By the time the craft fair rolled around she had twenty-three to contribute but decided to keep on making them for her parents' tree at home.

"I told you it was therapeutic," Gabby said.

"It just passes the time."

"Can we have a couple for the ward's tree, Bridget?"

"Sure. Take your pick."

"Can I have one to take home?"

"Sure."

Dr. Solomon, whom she hadn't seen since being told of her discharge, came around to take a look at her work. "These are just lovely."

"Ya want one?"

"I'd love to have one."

"Take your pick."

"Thank you, Bridget. You've got a wonderful eye. I'm sure you'll do very well in pottery."

"Pottery," said Bridget, looking up.

"Have you enrolled at the college yet?"

"No. I guess I better do that, eh?"

"I would think so. It must be getting rather late."

"Yeah, I'll do that."

"Are you looking forward to going home?"

"Oh, I dunno."

"I'm sure your family will be glad to have you back. Your Uncle Albert especially."

"Albert doesn't even live with us."

"Oh!" The doctor pursed her thin little lips. "I was given to understand that he did. He was so insistent you be sent home."

It was because Albert liked for people to be where they goddamn well belonged. He had been harassing the doctor, the nurses, and even Sylvia Plath ever since Bridget's arrival on the ward. Gabby had related that he would sometimes call up on the pretext of wanting to speak to Bridget and instead take the opportunity to blast whichever nurse picked up the phone.

"Hello, Four South."

"Is Bridget Murphy there, please?" Polite, older male relative voice.

"Yes, if you'll hold a . . ."

"Well Jesus liftin, when are you fag psychiatric sons of whores gonna let her out of that hell hole?"

"Would you like to speak to Bridget, sir?"

"I'd like to speak to her all right. I'd like to speak to her sitting in her own goddamn kitchen is where I'd like to speak with her, but I can't do that until you bastards decide to turn her loose — as if she's some kind of Jesus menace to society or something."

And of course the nurses, being psychiatric nurses, wouldn't be as quick to respond in the way that any one else in the same situation would, namely by hanging up on the raving old fart. They had been trained for every eventuality, and this sort of thing they were eternally ready for. The family was a volatile thing. The family, usually the organism responsible for the child's internment in Four South in the first place, could not normally be expected to comprehend why one of its number would need to be there. Bridget gathered that phone calls like Albert's were pretty much par for the course in Gabby's line of work. Leaning back in the chair and lighting a cigarette, whichever nurse was on shift would robotically switch into a mode of soothing reasonability once the first note of hostility had reached her ears.

"It's not that she's a menace to society, sir, that's not the case at all. It's just that she needs a bit of sheltering right now."

"Shelter she can get from her family!"

"No — obviously she can't or she wouldn't be here."

"What the eff is that supposed to mean?"

"I only mean that your daughter has come through a hard time, and often, following events such as these, young people need a period of . . . hibernation, if you will . . ."

"She's not my goddamn daughter."

"Oh. To whom am I —"

"This is her uncle, by God! Albert Patrick Murphy!"

"Well, Mr. Murphy, we do appreciate your concern."

"Yah, well, you may as well appreciate me hole for all the good it does."

Bridget often thought her uncle must be unique. He was the only man she knew who saved his temper for strangers rather than his family and friends and not the other way around. When she had lived with him and Bernadette, Albert would curse at the television news and its single mothers, "welfare sluts," simultaneously leaning over to pour Bridget more tea and berate the little bastard who was her undoing.

"You're a good girl," he would tell her over and over again. "You're a good girl and a goddamn smart girl and no little puke from Home Hardware is going to mess up a future as bright as yours, good girl." And Bridget would try for a couple of minutes to envision it.

Post card from Mona:
    WHAT I WANT TO KNOW IS ONLY THIS
    ONE THING: WHICH DO YOU THINK IS

WORSE: WHEN SATAN LOVES YOU OR
WHEN SATAN HATES YOU. AND ALSO:
WHICH DO YOU THINK IS ACTUALLY THE
CASE.

YOURS TRULY MONA.

PS IT'S THE SAME THING MAYBE.

CHAPTER 9

Archie Shearer's trial was only now beginning. Now. At Christmas, people emphasized. Sad for the family, they said, meaning the MacDonnells. And the thought of sad families at Christmas inevitably also brought to mind that of the gone Kenneth MacEachern. The state of the young people was freshly lamented. So much unhappiness brought upon the families. Killing each other and killing themselves.

The visitors, coming round the house all through the holidays, said that. There was teensy Mrs. Boucher rasping between drags on her Du Mauriers and kicking her dangling feet, which never quite reached the floor when she sat down. Back and forth, like an impatient six-year-old.

"It just make me sick," she would mourn, "all de det." Mrs. Boucher was a mournful woman, sickly, with a sad life. She'd slurp her tea, everybody aware of the fear she had for her married nineteen-year-old girl, in and out of the women's shelter every two or three months. Everyone in the house found themselves wanting to get things for Mrs. Boucher.

"I tell her, come home with me, Louise. No, Ma, I rather get the crap beaten out of me than live with my mudder like a little kid. Well, what do you do?"

Uncle Albert, down with Bernadette for the holidays, would nod soberly even though he wasn't. He was "back on it again," according to Bernadette, after thirty-three years. No one could really believe it. Apparently Albert had turned up with a bottle of Crown Royal one day last week and ecstatically poured himself three fingers in front of his wife. "'What in the Lord's name are you about with that?' I said to him. 'To hell with it,' he says, 'It's Christmas, the kids are all gone and I've been sober for thirty-three years. It's time to celebrate, Mommy!' And doesn't he gulp the christly thing down right before my eyes!"

Now everybody sort of had the feeling that they should behave very disapprovingly and discouragingly towards Albert every time he came out from underneath the sink with his bottle and a "Who wants a snoutful?" But with the exception of Bridget's father, no one could actually bring themselves to do it. He was too much fun. Except for putting him in perpetual good cheer and turning his cheeks and nose a welcoming pink, the liquor had no great effect on the man, certainly none of the adverse effects that everyone, for some reason, had been expecting. He was simply the same old Albert, spreader of good cheer, offering to replace Mrs. Boucher's tea with a hot buttered rum.

"No, it no good for my stomach, Ally."

"Ach, it's good for every goddamn piece a ya. A nice toddy, then, Marianne?"

"No, Albert, I just have more tea."

Which meant that Albert had to content himself with making a toddy for the priest, whom he did not approve of half as much as he did Mrs. Boucher, a woman who had spent six years of her life caring for Margaret P. in spite of her own hardships. Bridget could remember being small and sitting at the kitchen table at Margaret P.'s house with Mrs. Boucher, watching her smoke and listening to her tell ghastly tales about her no-good brudder. Her no-good brudder used to break into her apartment and steal the television set for booze. Her no-good brudder would threaten to beat her if she didn't give him money. Mrs. Boucher was so relieved to be working at Margaret P.'s, away from her no-good brudder, that she was almost sick. Bridget remembered trying to keep up by telling Mrs. Boucher about Gerard, who always beat her up and spit in her hair and wouldn't play with her. He had gotten hold of her Wonder Woman doll and sawed the top of its head off with a steak knife.

Father Boyle was, like Albert, another harmless and uninteresting drunk, but this did not stop Bridget's father from complaining about "the fat-arsed jeezless souse coming around to tell me I'm going to hell for forgetting to bless myself every time I sit down to take a shit" after each of his visits. To the best of Bridget's knowledge, Father Boyle had never said anything like this to her father, but any sort of moral authority figure was suspect in Bridget's father's eyes. He could not abide self-righteousness in any of its forms. Across the kitchen table, Bridget could see her father relishing the fact that Father Boyle had sat there and knocked back two of Albert's toddies since his arrival, ostensibly a visit to look in on Margaret P. "To look in on Mumma for a good two minutes before proceeding to drink us out of house and home" would be the comment later.

Albert was in a state that Bernadette cluckingly called High Gear, scuttling around to make toddies and pour tea for the guests when he wasn't darting down the hall to check on Margaret P.'s cheer, which lately hadn't been too bad. Margaret P. had taken to singing the song about the three Marys since Bridget got home, and despite the depressing lyrics, the singing seemed to keep her content and less likely to succumb to her usual macabre hallucinations. When Bridget first showed up, Margaret P. had been convinced that Bridget herself was one of these spectres, having returned from the dead after being shot by a boy. And this notion didn't seem to frighten Margaret P. in the least. She said, "Hello, dear. Are you still in purgatory?" and began to say a rosary. Since then, every time Bridget stopped by her room, the ancient thing would say nothing beyond holding up the rosary, shaking it encouragingly and calling, as though Bridget were far away, "It won't be long now, dear! You just hold on for a bit more."

"I'm not in purgatory, Gramma,"

"We'll get you up there, dear. I've lived a good life and they'll listen to me."

But Margaret P. had now forgotten about the continuous rosaries and replaced them with "Mary Hamilton" all day long. She sat, rocking back and forth and singing about the three Marys over and over again, a smile nestled somewhere in the folds of her face.

> Yesterday e'en there were four Marys,
> This night there will be but three.
> There was Mary Beaton and Mary Seaton
> And Mary Carmichael and me.

Albert and Bridget's father were pleased to hear the old lady singing after so long, but only Bridget seemed to recognize that Margaret P. had confused it for the rosary, that in her cobwebby mind she was still busy praying for Bridget's unworthy soul. And she must have considered it pretty unworthy because she hadn't stopped since Bridget got back.

Albert had been explaining all this to the priest and Mrs. Boucher, how Margaret P. had gotten it into her head that Bridget had been shot instead of Jennifer MacDonnell, careful not to let it slip that it had been Mrs. Boucher's gossip that set this delusion off. And this explanation had got them on to the subject of the dead, bemoaning particularly the young people and all the dying and killing they did.

"It's the parents!" Albert pronounced recklessly. High Gear had the effect of causing Albert to make reckless pronouncements throughout the day, ideas he might otherwise have made every effort to suppress in front of Bridget's father.

"It's not the goddamned parents," the latter countered at once. "I've never bought into that psychiatric-free-love-save-the-seals horseshit, and I'm not about to now. Blame everything on the parents, forget about personal responsibility. I say if some little bastard is gonna be a weirdo goon and pick up a rifle to shoot some young girl stupid enough to get tangled up with him, then that's what he's gonna do. And people encourage that now, anyway. They think it's *cool* to be wanting to do away with themselves or the young girls. It's in all the movies now, in the videos they watch. Well, I say let them kill themselves if they want to, but if they start aiming those guns at anyone else, by God, I'll hold the door to hell open for them and kick their arses on through."

Bridget's mother said, "Well, I didn't know Archie Shearer, but Kenneth MacEachern was in my grade six religion class and he was just a lovely lad. He told me that he wanted to be a priest."

"Oh yes, but the sons of bitches change once they hit their teens," Bridget's father said, happy to be angry and deliberately not checking his language in front of Father Boyle. "They get arrogant and start thinking they know everything and you can't tell them a goddamn thing after that."

All the proof he needed was, Bridget supposed, sitting at the table with him. He had made his disgust at both her and Gerard's respective betrayals known since the first day they had ever disagreed with him. Gerard had been about thirteen, Bridget a couple of years older, and their father had been so offended that he hadn't bothered to try and tell them anything since. Now, if he ever wanted to express displeasure at something they did, he pretended to agree with it — not speaking to them, but to the air. "Yes, that's what he wants to do," he would say, "he figures it's the right thing. Well, lord love a duck, isn't that just a dandy one. Well, why the hell *doesn't* he do it? A capital goddamn idea." Gerard could imitate their father at this with uncanny accuracy.

Bridget had to re-acclimatize herself to all the chaos she'd forgotten about, especially now that she had the empty, echoing ward to contrast it against. She had read somewhere that people who are colour-blind all their lives find it too overwhelming, once their eyes are operated on, to experience the world in colour. They loose all perspective and are terrified and lost and sometimes get physically sick. This was kind of what coming home was like, even though Bridget had spent all her life there and only four months on the ward. Coming out a far greater adjustment than going in had been.

She would sit and drink tea until about three in the afternoon and then switch to rum and eggnog before dinner, wine during, and anything else for the remainder of the evening. She could get away with this because it was Christmas and because everyone wanted her to be happy and content. She was genuinely pleased at how much easier it was to get drunk after four months abstinence, although it was not the same kind of drunk as before. It made her serene, content to be doing whatever it was she happened to be doing. If she was baking cookies with her mother, she was content to be doing that. If she was helping Margaret P. to the toilet, she was content to be doing that. Because her feeling was that really she *wasn't* doing that. This was a relief. She did not get edgy and excited like she used to and have to leave the house at two in the morning.

And nobody chastised her about anything. Her father did not even confide his displeasure to the air.

"What do you think Bridget? Didn't you know Kenneth? Or was it Archie Shearer you knew?"

A jolt. Bridget's mother had always been one to forget about spoken or unspoken household rules. Her father said she did it on purpose. When Bridget's father had decided a few years back that he was going to disown Uncle Albert and made it understood that no one in their family were to have any contact with him, Joan had forgotten all about this edict in the second week and ruined the effect by calling up Bernadette to make plans for a day of shopping at the Mic Mac Mall. So Bridget shouldn't have been surprised, really, that her mother would conformingly tip-toe around her for the first couple of days, clearing away her tea-cups, before absently letting drop a question about killing and dying.

"Bridey's one of the good ones, goddammit!" Albert interjected, pink-faced and reckless. She could hear the recklessness in his voice as he stood at the counter behind her, and she could feel everyone willing him to sit down and have a piece of bannock or something.

"God knows she could have taken the easy way out, or done something foolish or what-have-you." He came up behind her chair and Bridget could hear him swallow. She looked up at Gerard, who sort of smiled. He was leaning on his hand, fingers tapping against his head as if they were feeling for a trap door.

"We should just thank the Lord she had enough sense to do the right thing," Albert finished in an even louder voice.

"Yes, Bridget, you're a wise girl," Father Boyle agreed, being priestly in his attempt to save Albert from awkwardness.

"Goddamn right," Albert barked, repaying the Father with blasphemy. He gave Bridget a too-hard pat on her head.

Bridget's father looked at Albert for a little while to make sure he was finished speaking. "That isn't really what we were talking about, now, is it?" he said, at length. "That's not what I would call the issue at hand. I believe what we were talking about was a lot of jeezless punks who should all be sent to military school. That's all that's needed in this particular situation, the military would straighten them out pretty goddamn quick. They'd take that heavy metal horseshit, the army would, and all those big ideas about the world and how they should all kill the parents who feed them and grow their hair to their arseholes and be a bunch of faggots who don't have children but think they can adopt normal people's and eventually kill off the whole goddamn human race, the army would sew all that horseshit up into a tight little ball, stick it in a rifle and fire it straight up their shitty little arseholes, that's what a little discipline would do for those sons of whores."

"Oh, now," said Father Boyle, rousing himself a little. "My."

Between four and six in the morning, Bridget would dream she was still on the ward, packing to go home. She was feeling around in the ceiling for her stuff, but none of it was there. Instead she kept pull-

ing out handfuls of all these nonsensical items, all this crap. Car
alarms, even though she wasn't really sure what a car alarm would
look like. Plain donuts. The filter out of her mother's clothes dryer.
The head off a Barbie. And one morning at about eleven o'clock,
Bridget came downstairs to pour herself a cup of tea and her mother
told her that she had already come down four hours earlier. Bridget
didn't believe her. Joan said that Bridget had looked her straight in
the eye and demanded, "Where the hell is it?"

"It's up in bed, dear," Joan had supplied without batting an eye.
Maternal telepathy.

"Up in bed? Are you sure?"

"Yes, it's up in bed, dear, go on up."

"All right then!" Bridget supposedly had said, stomping back up
the stairs.

A lot of the time, she felt as if she were still on the ward. Sitting in
front of the television working on a snowflake, busier than ever at
these because her mother wanted to put them on all the Christmas
presents she gave out. And Byron was still around. Byron had sent
Bridget a Christmas card with a piece of paper inside, folded up as
many times as possible. It had writing on both sides as well as side-
ways, in the margins. It was completely covered with writing.

Bridget would have expected Byron's handwriting to be as inco-
herent as his mental state, but it seemed as though he had taken
pains for this not to be the case. He had meticulously printed everything in block letters, like a grade one teacher, which made Bridget
feel nostalgic as she read. And whereas Mona, in both letters and conversation, never once seemed to make reference to Bridget (even in the
note that had asked, "Which do you think is the case?" Bridget never
kidded herself that Mona was really asking *her*), Byron, on the other
hand, talked about Bridget all the time. About how she perceived and
felt about him. "YOU THINK I'M A GREAT GENERAL," part of
the letter said. "A GENERAL OF THE COSMOS. YOU FEAR
THAT TO LOWER YOUR WALLS IS TO INVITE DESOLA-

TION. THIS IS NOT SO. LIKE ALEXANDER, I CONQUER WITH ARISTOTELIAN WISDOM AT MY COMMAND. YOU FEAR ME LIKE AN UNTYABLE KNOT. YOU FEAR MY SO-LUTION."

She didn't know if that meant she feared him the way she would fear a knot that was untyable (why would she?), or if Byron actually meant that she feared him in the same way an untyable knot would fear him (how could it?). Bridget was embarrassed in any event and wondered if there was some way she could get him to stop writing without actually having to acknowledge his letters. She doubted that ignoring them would do it because he would just meet her silence with more grand surmises about what she thought of him. It was difficult dealing with someone like Byron. Near the end of her stay on the ward, she practically had to pretend to hate him in order to get him to stay away. A couple of times she was almost able to muster up the priceless mode of abuse that had overtaken her when Mona was around, but mostly all she could think to do was to call him an asshole. Paradoxically, though, simple little insults such as these seemed to get the better of Byron with even greater success than the more insightful ones did. Byron could never suffer to be called something so banal as an asshole.

"I know what you really mean!" he would holler, jumping on the furniture as he had taken to doing. "You mean that because I've read every book ever written and have a rudimentary knowledge of four different languages AT LEAST, my personality seems lofty and inaccessible to the average mind, perhaps even slightly disagreeable."

"I mean you're an asshole."

The band of disfunctionals that had taken to gathering in her room would typically guffaw at this sort of thing, Byron so horribly adept at setting himself up. But it still didn't get rid of him. He would sit there rocking back and forth on the opposite bed, his skinny legs folded underneath him, endlessly cajoling Bridget to admit that her hostility was really due to the fact that she felt dwarfed and belittled by his intellect, overwhelmed by his charisma.

Not that it had not dawned on Bridget long ago that the only way to keep Byron's imagination in check was to exhibit the nothing she felt. But it was then he would always go for the taco.

During her last few days on the ward, Byron had been insinuatingly nice. He quit trying to convince her of how she was and what she thought of him and just started trying to be nice. He loaned her a book on out-of-body experiences, and Bridget spent her last nights in the hospital bed lying on her back with her arms and legs spread out so that no part of her body touched any other part, trying to have one. The book said that you were supposed to say to yourself, I AM ALIVE. I HAVE POWER. IT IS REAL over and over again. She finally gave the book back to Byron and said it was bullshit.

"You're not doing it right," Byron said, making an effort not to sneer at her since he was trying to be nice.

"How can I not be doing it right? It says you're just supposed to lie there."

"When do you try to do it?"

"At night."

"Well, you're not supposed to do it when you're tired."

"I'm not tired,"

"Oh yes, you don't sleep. Well, there's your answer. You're always tired, you just don't feel it any more."

"I sleep some, in the morning, between six and nine."

"Not nearly enough," Byron clucked, Gabby-like.

"Well, it seems to be all my body needs at the present time."

"Sure, just like all your body needs to live on is Mars bars and potatoes."

This was the first time Byron had ever discussed any aspect of Bridget that didn't have to do with him. It gave her a start that he had been paying such close attention. That he knew about her Mars bars.

Byron revealing all the things he knew about her without trying in some way to relate them to himself was part of his attempt to be nice. He didn't understand that it made him creepier. One day Gabby had been trying to herd them upstairs to the Teen Lounge to work on the Christmas craft assembly line, and Bridget had been floundering for an excuse not to go, as the only reason she had started going in the first place was the snowflakes and now she had all the material she needed to make them in her room. So the excuse she came up with was it made her too depressed to see all the sick kids assembled up there with their IV poles and wheelchairs and withered or missing limbs. But it hadn't worked.

"I understand that, Bridget, I totally understand that," Gabby said, nodding at her and shooing her along at the same time. "But you have to realize that this is the world we live in and sometimes there are sad things in it. We all have to learn to face that."

And a few minutes later, as the herd trudged down the hall to-ward the elevator, a voice behind Bridget said, "It's just because you had a baby." And it gave her a start. It gave her a bigger start, the voice, the words, than anything had in a long time. It was Byron again. The fact that it was always Byron pushing these buttons she never knew were there was a constant exasperation.

She started walking backwards to look at him. "What do you mean?"

"That's why you can't stand to see the sick kids. Because you're a mother." The look on his face, his desperate attempt not to look malicious or clever for a change, but kindly and understanding, was entirely grotesque.

"But how do you know about that?" The other people they were walking with, Maria and Kelly and Shane and the bunch, glanced over at her with brief interest and then glanced away again as if to say, "Huh."

"I heard you talking about it."

"You did not. I didn't talk about it in front of you."

"To your mother, when you were admitted."

"When?"

Byron looked irritated. He was just trying to be nice, and now he was being interrogated.

"When you were first admitted," he repeated, peevish. "And you were in the TV room, waiting for Solomon."

"But you weren't there!"

"Yes I was" — Byron looked up all of a sudden, his thin pink lips making an o, like he had forgotten something — "I was. In the playhouse," he said.

The playhouse was another thing on the ward which didn't belong there, like the Lego blocks and the Snakes and Ladders. It had Smurfs all over it and was a thing children, rather than teenagers, were supposed to enjoy, although sometimes Jimmy would hide in it until someone entered the room so that he could pop out, whooping, and scare them. Shane in particular hated this, and always refused to go in to watch TV by himself. And Mona had used it to hide from Gabby. Being the only hiding place on the ward, however, it wasn't a very good one.

"What the hell were you doing in the playhouse?"

"I was just there," Byron said, still peevish. He didn't want to talk about himself for once. He wanted to be endearing.

"Beating off, probably," Bridget muttered.

"No," Byron said.

Bridget tried to remember the things she and her mother had talked about that day. She couldn't remember saying anything. She remembered laying her head in her mother's lap and hearing her mother's pigeon voice and then actually falling asleep for the five or so minutes it took for Solomon to show up. But now she saw that this was the kind of thing Byron did. He sat around in the playhouse, listening to people talk. All the time she had lived on the ward, she hadn't realized this. It had always been him doing the talking, she thought. And this revelation in combination with the niceness, the cloying, gruesome, ersatz attempts at niceness, did something to her image of Byron during those last few days on the ward. She wasn't as inclined to joke at the sight of him squeezing his head between his hands like it was one big zit, rocking back and forth in front of her.

He came up to her and said, "Will you write to me?"

"Probably not."

"Why? Why! I've been nice to you! I never went for the taco . . ."

"All week," she snorted.

"I've been nice to you!" he repeated. "I want to be friends!"

"How can we be friends? I haven't been nice to you at all. I don't like you . . ."

"Oh, come on, we've had some laughs . . ."

"Laughs? We've had some laughs?"

"We laugh at Gabby sometimes. And Solomon for sitting with her legs open. We always . . . talk together."

"There's, like, how many of us on the ward? Eight? Of course we all end up talking to each other. It doesn't make us friends any more than I'm friends with Shane."

Byron got mad then and stopped trying to be nice to her. It was her third-to-last day on the ward, and he ignored her for the duration. It made her nervous, for some reason, to spend a day without Byron always at her. If he knew what an effect he always has on me, Bridget thought, as someone who I am bored and annoyed by and have no affinity with in the least, he would be very impressed with himself.

But by the next day she had become used to it and wished Byron could have adopted this position towards her long ago. She sat in her room, peacefully constructing her snowflakes, Kelly and Maria drifting in every now and again to inform her about anorexic matters, such as how making yourself throw up every day will eventually cause your teeth to rot, so it is better to just not eat rather than eat and purge.

"Won't not eating make your teeth rot anyway?" Bridget wondered, and Kelly looked unsure, but Maria answered, "Yes. Just not as soon." Bridget thought that the way Maria said this gave even Kelly, her disciple of non-consumption, the creeps. She might as well have added, "and by then it doesn't matter anyway."

CHAPTER 10

Because Bridget never bothered unpacking in any systematic sort of way, she just took what she needed out of her suitcase as she needed it, she didn't find what Byron had left near the bottom of it until at least a week after getting home. It accounted for the sort of apologetic yet self-righteous you-did-deserve-it-after-all tone to his cramped letter.

> THE GREAT RABBI SAID: I HAVE COME TO
> START A WAR. HE PLUCKED OUT THE EYES
> OF SINNERS WITH HIS LEFT HAND AND
> BLESSED THEM WITH HIS RIGHT. I CALL
> THIS EQUITABLE.

In a single letter, Byron compared himself to Jesus, Aristotle, Peter the Great, Alexander the Great, Napoleon, Alistair Crowley, and someone Bridget didn't know named Mesmer. He also threw in Hitler at one point.

> ULTIMATE POWER WAS AN INEVITABILITY
> FOR HITLER — FOR HE WAS ULTIMATELY
> FEARED. SUICIDE WAS ALSO INEVITABLE —
> FOR HE WAS ULTIMATELY UNLOVED. MY
> ULTIMATE HOPE IS TO STRIKE A BALANCE
> BETWEEN THESE TWO, TO MAKE MYSELF
> LESS FORMIDABLE IN YOUR EYES AND
> THEREFORE DECREASE YOUR FEAR.

This was Byron still trying to be nice in his megalomaniacal way. And perhaps trying to make amends for the sperm all over her clothes.

"Mom, don't use the dishwasher, I need to do a load of wash."

"Oh, I can do that for you, dear."

"That's okay."

Although it would have been funny if she did. It was funny to imagine what her mother would have surmised at the load.

"The load," Bridget said to herself, measuring Tide. The interesting question was how he had done it. When had he done it? She had packed everything pretty much at once, the day she left. She zipped the bag shut and went to breakfast. But Byron had been at breakfast, alternately glaring and smirking. How long would it have taken? Could he have been sauntering down the hall on his way to breakfast and simply ducked into her room to relieve himself in just a couple of seconds? She supposed he could have, but she wasn't a hundred percent sure. She would have asked Gerard if she thought he could stomach it.

Gerard was a terrible hypocrite, really. He prowled around the house, bored, impatient to get back to school, and whenever he came upon Bridget he would tell her about his sexual conquests at the university and all the partying he did with the guys in residence. These guys had names like Killer and Toaster and Sniffer, they all ended with er. Gerard, Bridget gathered, was hugely popular up there. Women flocked to him, he said. "Women love me!" he would exclaim, overwhelmed. "And they're everywhere."

"Well, aren't you just King Shit. Have you come across this sweet virginal douche bag you've been touting for the last five years?"

Gerard's lips pursed into his I-need-a-clean-knife-for-the-Cheez-Whiz look. "These girls aren't like that. For the most part, they're all tramps."

Bridget laughed at the archaic word "tramps." It was her mother's word. Whenever her father called someone a whore, her mother always delicately corrected him with "Tramp, you mean." "What the

Jesus difference does it make!" her father would holler. Joan would contend that "tramp" was "nicer." Bridget always thought about hobos when she heard the word, which she supposed made her mother right about it.

Bridget observed, "Well, the fact that they're tramps doesn't seem to stop you from fucking them."

"Well, what else are you supposed to do with tramps!" Gerard said, turning moodily. Gerard thought of himself as the moral centre of the family and didn't like to be called on it.

Bridget later found herself thinking about this conversation, that there was something strange about it. She thought the subject matter was the sort that Gerard and the rest of the family would normally wear their toes out tip-toeing around. Except Gerard wasn't. He was going on about tramps and sex as though everything was normal between them. They rented a video the same night and stayed up late watching it, drinking beer. For no particular reason Bridget decided to say in the middle of it, "Lookee here, Gerard. I'm a tramp. I'm one, right? At least by your criteria, aren't I?"

Gerard turned his chair toward her a little but scarcely took his eyes off the TV. "No," he said. "I mean, maybe, once, you could have been called that. But not anymore." This was not exactly Gerard trying to be kind. This was the mathematics of Gerard's mind. She could almost hear the calculations going on.

"Why not?"

"Because . . . you're, like. Redeemed."

"How?" she asked, holding her breath at the word, at the thought.

"You're better now. You've, like. Learned your lesson," he said.

Bridget sat back in her chair, draining the bottle. Is that what it was, she thought.

He had fascinated her with the word for an instant. It was not something that had ever occurred to her before, that redemption could be the result of the whole blood-soaked business, that anybody, especially Gerard, could see her as having been cleansed by it all instead of dirtied, made upright instead of fallen. What a completely, blasphemously skewed idea! She could not begin to conceive of the mental callisthenics Gerard must have gone through in order to arrive at such a conclusion. Bridget was on the verge of laughing at him again, she was going to tell him that it was pathetic the way people turned themselves into knots trying to accommodate reality. She was going to do that, but then she found that she was touched and decided to let Gerard think what he wanted.

She couldn't help but marvel at people more and more, at their reactions to her, their ideas. The way they expected her to be and respond to things. It reminded her of Mark and some of the remarkable things he used to come out with once they both knew what was happening. Before she left for Albert and Bernadette's and everything was more-or-less settled, he had called her up and told her he was very sorry because she wouldn't be going to the prom. Bridget had sat there with the phone in her hand — it might as well have been a banana or something. The prom, she thought. What's a prom?

"I just really think it's unfair," he said.

"Good God, it doesn't matter to me," she replied. But Mark hadn't believed her. Nobody ever believed her about this sort of thing.

"It's not right," Mark insisted. "I'll be there, having fun . . ." he let himself drift off.

"*You're* going to the prom?"

"Yeah," he answered sadly.

"Well, don't worry about it. Have fun."

Mark didn't say anything. He's waiting for me to ask who with, she thought.

"Who with?"

"Oh, you don't know her. She's from Grand Anse."

For the rest of the day, Bridget had wandered around the house thinking about the word: prom. It was the strangest sounding word. Was it short for something? Promenade? That had to be it. This had never occurred to her before. Prom. It sounded like a *Star Trek* word. What's the prom setting on the sub-space emitter, Mr. Spock? Or the name of an alien. Prom, your planet is facing annihilation. You must let us evacuate.

Back then — and it was scarcely six months ago, she kept trying to remember that it was scarcely six months ago — Mark had two kinds of phone calls. Nice ones, like the prom call, and mean ones. The two were easy to distinguish, the nice ones coming in the late afternoon or early evening and the mean ones usually coming late at night when he knew she would be the only one awake. At first when she started getting the nice phone calls she had been very impressed and thought it meant she would not be getting the mean ones any more. He would talk about how he was in therapy and spending time with the brothers up in Monastery on the weekends and learning about himself and why he drank, et cetera. And he accepted everything and understood everything and knew that she had to do what she thought was right. Bridget had no reason not to believe these phone calls at first and always felt relief. He always ended the conversation by saying that this was the last time he would ever call her.

The mean phone calls wouldn't come until at least a couple of weeks after the nice ones, so you couldn't say he was not trying. And it had been so hard, Bridget hadn't known what to do or say because she didn't hate him, she didn't want to make him angry or hate her, but she didn't want anything to do with him, either. There was no way of conveying this. If she were to come out and say, "Mark, I don't care how you're feeling or what you're doing," he would become infuriated. So for a while she simply listened to everything he had to say and then said good-bye at the end of it. But this encouraged him to call again. It was impossible until the idea of going to Albert and Bernadette's had presented itself.

This was one of the mildest Decembers she could ever recall. It rained almost every day and the temperature scarcely went below zero. Uncle Albert hated it and her father, revelling as usual in his perversity, claimed to love the unseasonable sogginess. "Winter!" he would holler. "Who needs the frozen bastard!"

"Just some white stuff for Christmas, Robert."

"Ah, to hell with all that white Christmas bullshit! It's cold and it's miserable and everybody just pretends to like it because they want to be like everybody else." Then the two of them would go outside to hang lights in the rain and argue about it some more. Then they would come back in, wet and still arguing. Albert said that he saw some people in Halifax putting up all blue lights on their houses and it had looked very pretty, and Bridget's father asked him if he was out of his goddamn mind.

"Oh my, all blue lights! I suppose that's what all the arse-tits up there are doing these days, are they? All blue, for the love of God."

"Well, it looked nice, Robert!"

"Oh, I'm sure it did. They've got a flair for decorating up there, those types."

Albert giggled at him. Albert was especially annoying to his brother this Christmas because now that he was back on the booze his mood was perpetually good and he wouldn't fight any more. He would giggle at him instead, which he hadn't done for thirty-three years, and Bridget's father wasn't used to it.

"Hee hee hee, hee hee hee," her father would mimic, "just like one of those fat jeezless girls Rollie goes to school with."

"When's Rollie going to school see Emma?"

"Oh, there now, Albert, now you've got himself started with your foolish antics."

And Rollie, having got started, would question Bridget's father about school and Emma until Robert had to take him down to the basement to work on the sander some more.

"There now, sir. Let's have another one of the baby Jesus."

"Jesus Chris' Almigh'y," Rollie would say, accepting a block of wood.

Bridget's father had given her a couple of Rollie's statues. One blob was supposed to represent the Virgin and another was of the Virgin and Child. It was ironic, but she knew from experience that he didn't mean it to be. When she and Gerard were children, her father always made sure there were one or two religious pictures hanging on both their walls, and Bridget always got the Virgin, the Baby, or the Virgin with the Baby, whereas Gerard always got a grown-up Jesus doing stuff — cleansing the temple or showing Thomas the holes in his hands or what-have-you. Her father had this idea that girls liked Mary and boys liked Jesus just as girls liked Barbies and boys liked G.I. Joes. So he had picked out the Madonna blobs for Bridget merely on the assumption that they were the most appropriate choices. Gerard got "Jesus Heals the Sick."

"There," he said. "You two go upstairs and pray to those for a little while, see if that doesn't do ya any good."

Another thing he figured might do the two of them some good was to stand at the cash register down in the shop while he and Rollie laboured behind the partition to keep up with the growing demand for Christmas items. But Gerard always managed to get out of this duty by complaining that he was the one who had to go cut down the frigging tree and hang all the frigging outside lights practically all by himself. It wasn't true, but since Bridget wasn't making any complaints about it and Gerard was, the easiest thing was to let Bridget do all the downstairs work while Gerard lifted his weights in the attic.

Bridget knew why Gerard didn't want to work the register. It was all the people. He hated the town and he hated the people. Bridget never understood why this was Gerard had been the most popular boy in school ever since grade one and never got beaten up by anybody. He won the Award of Excellence in track and field and was on all the teams. She could understand why Mark hated the town and why Stephen Cameron and Daniel Sutherland, never able to set foot at a dance without being pummelled, would hate the town, but she could never understand this in Gerard. The town had been nothing but good to him. The only thing she could think was that it had to be his innate revulsion for any type of life outside himself.

So Bridget took the brunt of the personhood with only the counter and the register for protection. It didn't occur to anybody in the house that this might be a source of awkwardness for her — this didn't even occur to Bridget at first until the people who knew her started coming in. It was women, mostly, middle-aged, with faces that were wholly familiar to Bridget even though she didn't really know who they were. Mothers of classmates. Her mother would know their names, but she wouldn't. Some of them sang in the choir at church, went to say rosaries with her mother at the wakes. They were the kind of women who called you by name and always seemed to possess some little tidbit of knowledge about you. That you had broken your ankle last spring. That you got picked to play Mary in the Christmas pageant.

Bridget saw now that the tidbit of knowledge these ladies possessed about her was uniformly the same tidbit. Of course it wasn't really a tidbit at all. Their responses to her were to adopt either one of two attitudes, one a kind of dewy-eyed solicitousness wherein they called her "dear" a lot, and the other a more honest sort of aloofness which did not arise so much from disapproval as it did from the simple condition of not knowing what to say. The latter attitude was preferable, but the former occurred more often. Both types of lady seemed to find it in somewhat bad taste to have come across Bridget there on display along with the ducks and the Christmas Rollie-blobs and Mr. and Mrs. MacGillicutty.

Bridget called the school in Halifax after her first day of working in the shop, and they told her it was too late to apply for January.

Bridget's friend Heidi came in. She flounced down the stairs and then froze in a posture of utter shock — mouth open, eyes wide, a caricature of someone stumbling into a surprise party.

"Omigod. I heard you were home and I couldn't believe it."

"Well, it is Christmas."

"Why didn't you call me? There's been three parties in the last week."

"Well, I don't want to go to any friggin parties, Heidi."

"You're such a bitch!" Heidi laughed then and twirled around on her toes for something to do. Bridget had always been able to be utterly blunt around Heidi. "You could have called, anyways."

"I don't like talking on the phone."

"Jesus Murphy, woman! Then you come over to the house!" Heidi paused to pretend she was an airplane. She spread her arms straight out and swooped back and forth in front of the counter, humming. Then she stopped abruptly and stared at Bridget.

"Omigod. You will not, will not, will not believe who I saw at Troy Bezanson's last weekend."

"I don't want to know, Heidi."

"Stephen Cameron!"

"Oh yeah."

"He's lucky he didn't get the crap kicked out of him. Drunk! I guess to Jesus he was drunk."

"Did Troy throw him out?"

"No, no, everyone else was three sheets to the wind and didn't give a shit. Troy goes, What the hell, we're all adults now."

"Huh."

"He was even kind of charming for a while there. Stephen reaches this point, like, around the fifth or so drink, where he just forgets all about that moody, the-world's-a-piece-of-shit bullshit and lets it all hang out. Joking and having a ball. I can almost tolerate him at that stage."

"So you're thinking . . ."

"I'm thinking it might be something to do for the winter. He's even got some muscles from working over at Hardware. Oh, but I don't know. Down goes the eighth drink or so and it's back to the gloom and doom times two."

"Yeah, he's a serious type."

"Going on about you and Mark . . ." Heidi slipped in, resuming her airplane.

"I don't want to hear about that."

"Mostly you. I think he figures he's your white knight."

"I don't care, Heidi."

"What are we on the earth for, he says, if not to help our fallen brethren? Brethren. Aren't we all fallen in some way? Didn't Christ consort with prostitutes, he says to me, sloshed all to shit."

"Jesus Christ."

"Well, that's what I said. Look here, you, I said to him, that's my friend you're talking about, and what happened to her could happen to any one of us. There but for the grace of God go I, and all that."

"And what did he say, Heidi?"

"He said, that's exactly what I'm talking about. Omigod, and then do you know what he did?"

"No."

"Puked."

"Oh."

"Nobody really cared, though."

"Did he get any on you?"

"No! I woulda clocked him one!"

"Well, that's good."

Heidi began to browse the shelves, picking up the occasional duck, the occasional golf ball. "Dad wants one of your father's ducks for Christmas. They're too friggin expensive, between you and me."

"Dad says I can take ten percent off for my friends."

"Oh, whoop-de-shit. Scarcely puts a dent in it. Well, I'll tell you something, Lady Jane," Heidi said, scrutinizing a polished piece of driftwood. "You could have called me or something and let me know how you were doing, in the last little while. Answered my letters."

Bridget knew that Heidi hadn't really cared about how she was doing. She had just wanted to know, to possess the knowledge that no one else had. This didn't make Heidi a bad person, because people were like that. It was natural. People never want anything except to have power, and that's what knowledge about others gives them, or so they think. She had figured this out from Byron, it was why Byron had to delude himself that he understood everything about everybody. Bridget now believed that most people couldn't tell the difference between wanting knowledge for power and wanting knowledge out of concern. Bridget didn't actually believe there was a difference. That was why she supposed that Heidi had a right, of some sort, to feel hurt not to have been told of Bridget's doings. Or at least had a right to feel thwarted in some respect.

Bridget used to think that Heidi was strange, the way she airplaned about and performed little dances down the halls at school and went from one topic of conversation to its polar opposite without scarcely taking a breath. And a couple of years ago Bridget had told Heidi about how, when she was four, she began to choke on a clump of spaghetti and almost died, and Heidi had laughed her hole out over this. Bridget used to think all this was strange, but even stranger was the fact that nobody else did. Heidi had never been picked on or ostracized in her whole life and was instead friends with, literally, everyone. Even those who were picked on and ostracized by everybody else, Heidi spoke to and hung around with. People the most popular kids would never have gone near, people like Stephen and Daniel, were all included among Heidi's acquaintanceship. Bridget never understood it: how Heidi could airplane down the halls and hang around with the likes of Alison Knofftall (Alison Snotball) and still be welcomed into all circles, while someone like Stephen Cameron, who was merely pale, and Daniel Sutherland, who was merely gangly, had been pariahs ever since grade seven.

"It's a guy thing," Bridget remembered Dan Sutherland saying once. "Guys decide who's popular and who's not. If you've got breasts and weigh under one hundred and thirty pounds, you're not likely to find yourself an outcast. If, however, you are a male with good grades and interests that do not even remotely involve a jock strap or helmet or stick of some kind, you may as well get all your teeth removed at the dentist's in advance."

Bridget never understood how this kind of thing worked. She had been friendly with a few people in high school but not close to anyone until she started seeing Mark and ended up being friends with his friends. She remembered a time just before they had started going out when they were only beginning to know each other. It had

been the only time in Bridget's life when the house was going to be
empty for a weekend — Margaret P. had to go to Halifax for tests of
some nature and the whole clan trekked to the city to be with her.
But Bridget hadn't been able to go because of school, and so she
took advantage of this unprecedented occasion to invite everybody
she could think of to come to her house and get drunk. This included Mark and Daniel and Stephen and some of the other guys.
Bridget had found it difficult that night to keep track of them
amidst all the bodies and the chaos and with trying to keep people
from having sex and smoking hash in her parent's bedroom, and
near the end of the evening when she went to look for the group of
them they were nowhere to be found. Monday she found out that
Troy Bezanson and Donnie Red Ferguson and Andrew Petrie had
chased them all the way down Cosgrove Street and kicked the shit
out of them. And Mark hadn't spoken to her for a week because he
figured that Bridget should somehow have known this would happen. Maybe she should have.

"Do you know," said Bridget to change the subject, "that I've
been sober for the whole four months I was at the Children's?"

"I didn't think the place had a bar anywhere."

"No, but I could have, though. Steve and Dan brought me in a
pint."

"Well, God love 'em. What did you do with it?"

"I still got it."

"Bring it over tonight."

Bridget was sorry she mentioned it. "No, I don't wanna go out . . ."

"Oh, come on, it'll just be me and you and Mum. She made a big
batch of Irish creme."

"She made it?"

"Yep."

"You can make that stuff yourself?"

"Sure you can. It's some friggin good, too. Come on over and
have some."

"I don't know — maybe later in the week."

"It'll be Christmas friggin Eve later in the week!"

Bridget felt hot and awkward, remembering how impossible it was to be evasive with Heidi. And Heidi would have a couple of drinks and then want to start talking about things. Heidi might say that it would be just the two of them, but the social animal in her could never be kept at bay for very long. She would start making flirty phone calls, winking at Bridget as she poured innuendo into the receiver, insisting they go out and meet such-and-such at the tavern. It would probably be poor Stephen, this time around. Stephen who, for all his world-hurt and cynicism, could never quite conceal the fact that not once in his entire high school career had he been the recipient of female attentions. It used to make Bridget depressed at Dan's parties to see Stephen, dressed entirely in black, not uttering a word as Heidi airplaned past to snatch the screwdriver from his white, unyielding hand. Heidi thought it was hilarious. Stephen said he thought it was hilarious, too, and would shuffle off to the kitchen to make himself another.

"I can't tonight," Bridget said with what she hope sounded like finality.

"Tomorrow night then," said Heidi with even more finality. "I'll call ya." She zoomed off up the stairs.

Bridget supposed that her problem was ambivalence. She didn't particularly want to see Heidi, but she couldn't be bothered fending her off. And when she had talked to Heidi about going out, she was convinced that it was the last thing she wanted to do. But more and more since she had been home with everybody, she was finding that leaving the house was all she could think of.

So she was at an impasse. And that was what it had always been like before. She could never get out of the house enough, and for a while it seemed as if Mark was her only way out of the house. Then it became the case that she couldn't get away from Mark fast enough, and the house was the only place where he couldn't get to her. So she saw now that it was hopeless and it didn't matter what she did. There would always be people, inside and outside, always at her.

Bridget had a nightmare about the Christmas turkey. It was the first frightening dream she could remember since the other sort-of nightmare about Kelly's angel-food cake. Her father had just cut into the bird when it leaped off the table, still hot and crackling from the oven, screaming "Don't you dare! Don't you dare!" Trailing stuffing across the kitchen floor.

One of those dreams where she was able to tear herself awake before it could scare her anymore. She made herself get out of bed. It was 8:25 in the morning, and she stood there in a softened beam of sunshine, filtering in through the patterned curtains, illuminating the floating dust. Christmas light, warming her. The words in her head were: How do you be dead? — which was the first thing she had thought after The Birth. But it hadn't really been a thought at all. It was bigger. It was this primal, fundamental wish that the sentence didn't do justice to. The word that came closest to doing it justice wasn't even God. There was no word. Just this prehistoric need to turn herself off. There had been crying (not from her, the wah-wah), and heated sheets which felt so good and people saying she could hold it, hold him, hold the wah-wah, and all she could think about was this thing she wanted that wasn't even God.

Help God No she thought now, standing in the muted sunshine.

Her mother made her sick. Her mother and her maternal telepathy had almost at once discerned the fact that Bridget's bowels were no longer moving. After a solemn conference with Aunt Bernadette, the retired nurse, Epsom salts were decided upon.

"I told them to give me Epsom salts at the hospital and they wouldn't," Bridget told them, as if to imply that if the doctors, in all their wisdom, hadn't felt it necessary to cure her with Epsom salts, perhaps the wisest thing was to just let nature take its course.

"I feel fine," she added.

"When was your last bowel movement?" demanded Bernadette.

"Um. I can't really remember."

"She can't remember."

The day went black. Bridget could not leave the bathroom for hours.

"Do you want a *Reader's Digest*, dear?" her mother called through the door.

"I can't read, Mother, I'm suffering."

"Heidi called for you, dear."

"Tell Heidi I expect to be on the toilet for the next few days."

"We could bring the phone in to you, if you like."

"I can't talk and shit at the same time, mother. It's uncouth. How would you like it if someone was shitting while they were talking to you on the phone?"

Bridget heard her mother shuffle away, tittering. Her mother was the only one to laugh at this thing. Albert and her father were very grave and Bernadette solicitous and nurse-like and Gerard thoroughly revolted. But her mother brought her tea and toast afterwards, humming and cracking jokes to herself.

"Here you go," she said. "Might as well start filling up the tank!"

"I don't ever plan on digesting anything ever again."

"You have to, dear. It's nature. I don't know what those doctors were thinking of. Don't you want your curtains open?" She stood up to open them, humming something and smiling.

"What are you saying, Mumma?"

"The worms crawl in, the worms crawl out, they eat your guts, and shit 'em out! We used to sing that when we were kids. I always thought it was so funny. Oh, I got in so much trouble with my dad!"

"That's not funny at all, Mumma, it's morbid."

"Yes, but the word 'shit,'" her mother explained with typical patience.

CHAPTER 11

Maria the slow-walking corpse, Maria the human question mark. Falling-out doll hair and big teeth. Goldfish eyes. Wrote an illiterate Christmas card.

> *Hello Bridget. I am home for X-mas. My famly dont try to make me eat becas they no I wont anyway. Kelly was discharjed and Byron was discharjed, but they are still outpatients. Kelly sed Byron wants a date, and she mite!*
>
> *Everyone els gets discharjed but I never get discharjed. Kelly has to see a nutrishonist (spelling?) and gos on her own. She folows a meal plan now. I will never do it.*
>
> *Solmon sed I couldnt go home for X-mas without eating a hole meal, so I had to do it. Gabby wouldnt let me go to the bathroom. I hat them. I hope you are having a good X-mas well by-by now Bridget.*

The first thing she thought was that it was funny Maria could spell outpatients but not nutritionist.

Maria holding a pencil in her fist sounding out words. Drawing rather than writing them. Had to eat a hole meal. No puking it up. She hats them.

Why not stick the pencil in her neck? In that yielding, oval space at the base, between the two bones. Didn't it even occur to her?

Bridget used the diarrhea excuse to stay in bed for a little while. Her mother brought the Christmas card up on a tray with ginger ale.

"Who's that from?"

"Maria. Anorexic."

"Is she better?"

"No. Home for Christmas."

"Eating?"

"No, Mumma, no, she doesn't eat. That's her thing."

Bridget's mother went to open the curtains again. "Poor wee thing. I wish I was with her right now."

Bridget's mother would sing "Mama's Little Baby Loves Shortenin' Bread" to Maria. But Mama's little baby didn't love shortenin' bread.

Bridget's father heard them through the wall.

"That girl gets hungry enough, she'll eat!" he hollered. "I know how to get a girl to eat!" Pretending to be hollering at no one in particular. He said the same thing about Bridget and her sleeping. Someone gets sleepy enough, they'll sleep, he'd tell the ceiling.

"It's not true," said Bridget.

"I know how to get a girl to eat! Keep her away from the goddamn cupcakes and chocolate bars, that's how you get a girl to eat."

And someone gets constipated enough, thought Bridget, exhausted inside of her body, they'll shit.

"If that girl were here now, I'd have her eating, by the Jesus," said her father, messing around with Christmas presents in the next room. Her father thought Maria was just being stubborn. Which Maria was. He trundled into Bridget's room with an armload of parcels, trailing paper and ribbon. "Here now," dumping them onto the foot of her bed. "You do these up all nice for Dad. Don't look too close at that there one. Mother, you get out of here, now, yours is there too."

"I'm sad for that girl," said her mother, just standing there.

"She's only got herself to blame," said her father.

Maria, aspiring cadaver. Studying for the corpse-hood. And Kelly the angel on earth, Kelly the blonde fairy. Mona the creature. Plump pink sweating mud beast, swinging tampons by their string in conversation. And Jennifer MacDonnell is now a thought. She's only got herself to blame. Bridget stayed in bed in her room for days until she got called down to have supper with everyone because it was Christmas Eve.

Bridget came down in her pyjamas and her father sent her back up to change. Her father was finding his footing with her again, slowly. With every edict to wrap Christmas presents or change her clothes or pick up her own goddamn tea cups he regained the old confidence. He had been brooding for the last couple of weeks. He was a man who attributed deviation from the normal mode of behaviour to just stubbornness. As with Maria. He had the cure for stubbornness, he believed. Stubbornness, in his mind, was eminently curable when Robert Michael Murphy was present to take it in hand. You kick their shitty arses into gear is what you do. Bridget was too stubborn to sleep. Bridget was too stubborn to take a dump. Bridget was keeping it all inside out of sheer perversity. Bridget should have bounced right back from that nastiness in August. Now, Bridget should be properly penitent. But Bridget was too stubborn to be properly penitent and instead spent all her time stubbornly wallowing in whatever it is she was wallowing in. Bridget was too stubborn to be the happy laughing girl she used to be who laughed on his knee and fell asleep on his belly and felt so much guilt for eating a piece of licorice in church that she ran away and hid in the priest's woods overnight, hoping to die. Bridget was too stubborn to stay a child. Bridget's arse needed kicking into gear no matter what the commie fag psychiatric sons of whores might have to say about it. Bridget was home now, after all.

Rollie liked Bridget, and Bridget's mother sat them across the table from one another so that Rollie could look at her and smile. He showed her the fingers of his right hand, the nails almost bitten away, the cuticles in shreds. Joan had put bandages on a couple of them.

"Not lookin so good there, Roland."

"Oh — now how am I supposed to eat?" Gerard complained. Gerard expected Christmas dinner to be nothing but one big gross-out after another and had loaded up on biscuits and cheese and mandarin oranges beforehand, knowing he'd lose his appetite any way.

"Try to break his nails, Bri-het," Rollie said, regarding them closely, to tease her.

"You leave those nails alone, you."

Rollie smiled at the reproach and the hand disappeared under the table.

"Where you goin Bri-het?"

"I'm not going anywhere."

"Hal-fax."

"I'm not going to Halifax."

He put his hands over his ears and rocked a little.

Rollie had a cold and the family was trepidatious about his nose running at the table. Rollie was always equipped with Kleenex in his front pocket, but often he didn't think to use it and just let things hang. Nobody wanted that to happen. Joan and Robert checked him regularly and Gerard went out of his way not to. This was their life. Checking for leaks. Margaret P. was another one for the Kleenex, always needing to hork. She kept a little plastic bag by her side at all times to deposit the dirtied ones into. A plastic bread-bag, provided by Joan. Bridget would forever associate these things with Margaret P. — balled Kleenex and bread-bags. And diapers, plastic sheets and bedpans. Things having to do with her leaks. All of Margaret P.'s friends and family who would have remembered her as fun or as smart or as wilful or as a fine person, they were all dead, all of them, because Margaret P. was almost one hundred. The last people to remember Margaret P. on earth would be people who knew her as a series of leaks that needed stopping up.

Bernadette helped Margaret P. to the table — she came farting — and Joan set the food out. Albert was circling the table with a drink in one hand and a bottle of Black Tower in the other, pouring for everybody, in High Gear and not wanting to sit down. Robert watched TV until the last possible minute because Joan got mad at him if he started poking around the kitchen eating while she was trying to get everything ready.

"Who's that?" said Margaret P., squinting, balanced in her chair.

"It's Bridget, dear," hollered Bernadette. "Home for Christmas."

Bridget was braced for a round of "Mary Hamilton" or an inquiry into the comforts of purgatory, but all Margaret P. said was, "Is she what stinks?"

"Yes, it's me," hollered Bridget, before any one else could say anything. "I'm what stinks."

Margaret P. peered at her, satisfied, while Bernadette used a fork to turn the old monster's dishful of potatoes, turkey, and cranberry sauce into a pinkish sort of paste.

Bridget's father waited until every one had loaded up their plates and taken their first couple of bites of food before launching abruptly into grace. He liked to see them all guiltily put down their forks and try to pray around a mouthful of stuffing. For the first time ever, Albert, drunk, whirled around and accused his brother of doing this to them every holiday, on purpose, just to be even more of a self-righteous old bugger than he already was.

"It's not my fault you're all a bunch of jeezless pagans who don't know to thank the Lord for what ya got."

"I'd like to think I thank the Lord every day, in my own way," said Bernadette. Bernadette was responsible for helping Margaret P. get the fork up to her mouth, taking turns with Joan. She held a paper towel in the other hand to catch whatever fell out.

"God bless you, Bernadette, yes you do, but I'm sure you'll agree some people seem to figure the way to thank the Lord for thirty-three years of sobriety is to go get liquored and act the fool on our Lord's own friggin birthday."

"Ah, Jesus," was all Albert could think to say.

"That's who we're speaking of, bye. And you'd do well to think more on him."

"Oh, yes. Yes, now. And some of us would do well to think less that they *are* him." This was spoken awkwardly, the last part muffled by food, so Robert wasn't able to come up with an appropriate response.

Bridget felt her stomach contracting on the second bite. She had been living on nothing but ginger ale and toast for the last couple of days. It wasn't going well. Her stomach was being stubborn. Her stomach needed its arse kicked. She put her fork down.

"And what's your trouble?"

"Still not feeling well."

"Ach, you're stomach's just not used to it. Best thing to do is keep eating."

"I don't know about that, now," said Bernadette, the nurse.

"She needs some solid goddamn food in her for a change."

Margaret P. spat out a mouthful of potatoes. "Poison," she opined.

"Jesus Murphy, Ma, that's good goddamn food you're spitting out. Joan spent all day on that, now."

"Rollie," barked Margaret P. "Don't you eat that food. Don't let Rollie eat that food, now."

"He wants to eat," said Rollie, indignant.

"Wipe your nose, for Christ's sake."

"Jesus Chris' Almigh'y," said Rollie, touching his front pocket.

A few moments of awkward, cherished silence went by as every one chewed. Soon Margaret P. began to cry in the senile, affected way she had. Heaving great, artificial, gut-wrenching sighs. Every one listened to her.

"Margie, stop, now, dear," said Joan at last.

"I don't want Rollie to die," she said. "Bridey C. poisoned the food before she died."

"Goddammit, Ma, nobody poisoned the goddamn food, and nobody died."

"It's full of the cancer."

"You eat that, now, that's good food!"

"He wants to eat," said Rollie, really alarmed now. He listened to his mother over any one else.

"Then eat, for the love of God, nobody's stopping you. Mumma, you're spoiling our nice Christmas."

"Don't say that to the poor old soul," said Joan.

Albert leaned forward, trying for inconspicuousness. "Wipe your nose, Rollie, dear," he said gently.

"Well," said Gerard, "I'm done."

Bridget darted to the bathroom just seconds before Rollie sneezed onto his plate and the table exploded. Margaret P. began to sing about salt cod, trying to get the noise of them all out of her head.

She and Rollie sat together on the couch watching Judy Garland sing "Have Yourself a Merry Little Christmas" to a small child. It was very sad. Bridget didn't know the song was meant to be that sad. Nobody sang it that sadly any more. It was like when her father used to go around singing "Mary Hamilton" as if it were a bawdy song — "There was Mary Beaton and Mary Seaton and Mary Carmichael and me! Haw haw haw" — and not about a fourth, dead Mary at all.

Neither of them felt good. They had been given hot toddies.

"He's got the cold," remarked Rollie. "Got the head cold in his chest."

"Wipe your nose. Wipe your nose, Rollie, don't just keep touching your pocket."

Rollie kept wanting Bridget to say, "Stop it." It was his favourite game. It wasn't really a game at all. He kept insisting she say "Stop it," and she would say it, and he would make her repeat it over and over again. It started when Bridget was two years old, so she was told. Rollie used to come over to the playpen when she was watching *Mr. Dress-Up* or something and pinch her arm to get her attention. And one day it must've smarted because Bridget turned around and whined, "Stoppp itttt!" And that was the way Rollie always wanted her to say it. He would always repeat it for her, imitating a high-pitched, baby-Bridget voice, until she got it more-or-less right. Sometimes Bridget could do this for him for hours and other times she had no patience for it. Tonight, she did it as much as he asked.

"How's Bri-het say stopppp itttt?"

"Stoppp itttt."

They sat in the light of the Christmas tree, which was covered with paper snowflakes.

"Stopppppppp ittttttttt."

"Stopppppp ittttttttt."

"Try to break his nails."

"He better not break his nails. Bri-het will give him a whuppin."

Rollie looked at her slyly. "Stopppp ittttt."

"Stoppp ittttt."

"How Raw-hurt say stop it?" This was one of Rollie's favourite jokes.

"Raw-hurt doesn't say stop it and you know it, Roland."

"No Raw-hurt don't say stop it Raw-hurt don't say hit." The very notion made Rollie titter to himself for a while longer. Then it would begin all over again.

"How Bri-het say stopppp ittttt?"

"Stopppppppppp ittttttttttttt."

"Stopppppp ittttttt . . .?"

"STOPPPPPPPPPPP ITTTTTTTTTTT."

"Goddamn cuckoo's nest," she heard her father mutter, full-mouthed, from the kitchen. Sitting alone with a plateful of leftovers.

Phone rang.

"What are you up to now?" he said.

"Just sitting here with Roland."

"How is the old retard?"

"He's got the cold."

"Got the cold, does he. I hear it's been going around."

"Yes. That time of year."

Breathe, breathe. Bridget had to go to the bathroom again. Her bowels twisted.

"Well, I suppose I just called to say Merry friggin old Christmas."

"Thanks."

"What about you, what do you have to say?"

"Merry Christmas to you."

"I guess you're home for good, now, are ya?"

"I don't know about that . . ."

"Yah. But probably you are."

Her stomach made a noise. She heard him sniff. "Probably you are," he said. "I don't suppose you heard that my granddad died the other day."

"Yah, Mom said something."

"She was at the wake."

"She goes to all the wakes."

"Yah, well, it wasn't exactly what I needed to see at that particular point in time, if ya know what I mean."

"She goes to all the wakes, though."

"Well, isn't she good."

Bridget looked over at Rollie and gave him a swat to get his fingers out of his mouth. "Sorry about your granddad, though," she said finally.

"You're sorry, are you?"

"Yes."

"Well, fuck me if that doesn't make it all better."

Maria in her thoughts all day and still was. Closed her eyes on the toilet in contemplation of Maria. Maria's shape untwisting itself from the big question mark it used to be in Bridget's mind. Maria standing apart from everything. Maria would not go to parties she didn't want to go to. Maria would not cry at the sight of a cake. Maria was resolute, always. Maria did not know guilt. Maria would never feel sorry for those who had made her life difficult. Maria would never give in to bribes or begging or be moved by someone else's pain. You could lead Maria to water, but you could not make her drink. You could stick tubes into Maria's hands and arms to pump in glucose, but it wouldn't count. Maria would always win out.

Braced against the inexorable will of mankind, of God and of nature, Maria comes out on top. Disintegration on her own terms, Bridget thought. She had used to think Mona was the powerful one, but that was just because Mona was big and loud. Maria had the strength of the invisible. Mona just had bluster. Mona blustered and blew until her German father had enough of her and picked her up and plunked her down again elsewhere. Mona would always be happy and sad, happy and sad like that.

CHAPTER 12

Not only was Bridget dead, but she stank, according to Margaret P. This was all anybody heard about on Christmas Day. Margaret P. was adamant about it every time Bridget came into her foggy line of vision.

"What stinks?"

"Nothing stinks, Mumma." Albert, gentle.

"Is that Bridey C.?"

"Yes . . ."

"Then she's what stinks."

"Mumma, is that nice?"

Margaret P. would look at him in honest wonder. "I'm not saying it to be nice, Albert. Can't you smell it? Something needs to be done."

There was a snow storm, finally, which covered everything up and Bridget went out and walked around in it, blind with the white. The wind whipped the fine snow about in sheets but was not devastatingly cold. Bridget walked to the wharf and on the way she could vaguely see the Christmas lights on people's houses. The unfrozen strait was grey and seething.

Her Christmas presents had been bath beads and bath salts and perfume that smelled like bacon fat to her, so maybe she did stink. Bernadette had given her a gaudy makeup kit shaped like a seashell and inside were ten different kinds of eye shadow. Twenty bucks from Margaret P. Teddy bear from Albert, one of the fancy, expensive kind like they sold in the hospital gift shop. Plush and fuzzy with horrifyingly real eyes. Pink bow sewn to its head. Snowboots from the folks, which she now wore. "Rebecca Wipes the Forehead of Jesus" from Rollie.

Bridget plowed through the snow drifts toward the church, to see it lit up, and the manger, which she realized half-way there would be completely covered with snow. None of the roads had been plowed yet, nor had the church parking lot, so making her way across it was a trial. The drifts came up to her waist. The wind was so strong that when she turned around to see the path she had made through the expanse of white, it had pretty well disappeared as if she hadn't been there. Bridget thought that snow drifts and the sand dunes you saw on television looked the same. It made her think about the poem the nurse had given her at the grown-up hospital, the poem she saw everywhere, on calendars, on the walls of doctors' and dentists' and priests' and veterinarians' offices. About the guy at the end of his life seeing two sets of footprints in the sand, and the other set was supposed to be Christ's. And at certain points, at the hardest parts of his life there was only one set of prints. And when he asked Christ what the deal was with that, Christ replied, "That was when I carried you." Bridget thought, Why would this nurse give her a poem she saw everywhere she went anyway?

Heidi wanted Bridget to go out on Boxing Day so Bridget was practising being out. Once she had finished cutting her futile swathe across the parking lot, she decided to plow through it a second time. Just for the hell of it. Just for the halibut, Albert would say.

"I saw you," Daniel Sutherland said to her, "walking back and forth across the church parking lot the other day."

"Yesterday," said Bridget. "Christmas Day."

"In the snow storm."

"Where were you?"

"I was at the Petries' with my parents. All they had to drink was eggnog. I was on an eggnog drunk. You get this sugar buzz."

"What's James Petrie doing these days?"

"I don't know, I didn't ask."

"I heard he had some kind of nervous breakdown."

"That's why I didn't ask. At first I wasn't sure that it was you. You had your hood up."

"Yes."

"But then I thought, who else could it be?"

"Did anybody else see me?"

"They all saw you."

"Dandy."

"They thought maybe it was you, but they weren't sure."

"What did you say?"

"I didn't say anything."

Dan and Bridget threw beer caps at each other, sitting on the living room floor with their legs splayed out, beer bottles in front of each of them. Stephen Cameron was looking at her from the couch with Mrs. Boucher eyes.

"What did they say?"

"They said, Poor Bridget Murphy."

"Jesus, Dan," said Stephen Cameron.

"Poor Bridget Murphy," said Bridget. She was beating Daniel badly. His family had gone to see their relatives in Dominion, and he had been smoking weed out of an old man's pipe all day. He wore a bowler hat while he did this, and the effect was comical.

"You're a comical old bastard," said Bridget. "I want some eggnog, right now."

Heidi slid down the banister, coming from the bathroom. "Omigod," she said. She flopped on the couch and put her legs across Stephen Cameron's lap. "Do you remember the time you puked in the plant?"

"I think I puked under the plant."

"No," said Daniel. "You puked in the plant, I remember because it died."

"You'd think it wouldn't die from that," said Bridget.

"My mom was mad," said Daniel.

"I'm sorry."

"No, no, who gives a shit, puke in it again. We're all adults here."

"How's things up at Dal, anyways?"

"Disconcerting," said Daniel. "To think I may not be as smart as I thought I was. Although I'm still fairly sure that I am."

"Well, that's good."

"Nobody's as smart as they think they are, that's something I've learned," said Stephen Cameron. Heidi began kicking him rapidly in the thigh.

"Lighten up! Remember what I told you about lightening up?"

Bridget wasn't having fun, but she was almost as drunk as she could possibly be. There had been other people around, but they had gone off to the tavern hours ago. Now Heidi wanted to go to the tavern, and Daniel said he would only go if he could wear his hat. Stephen said he would get beaten up if he wore his hat, and Daniel argued that they were going to get beaten up anyway. "You see?" he said to everyone. "I've been taking logic at school."

"No one is thinking about Bridget," Stephen said at last.

"Bridget likes it that way," said Daniel.

"Omigod, Bridget doesn't give a shit," Heidi said.

"That's right, don't worry about me."

"Well, I'm only saying guess who might be there."

"The Guess Who might be there?" said Daniel.

Stephen made her go into the bathroom with him. Daniel's mother had put bowls of decorative soap everywhere. The room smelled of them.

"Melodrama," said Bridget.

"I'm only saying I don't know if we can protect you if anything happens," he said. He kept trying to put his hands on her arms, and Bridget kept reaching up with her forearms to push them off. It was a neat little trick.

"Things are different," said Bridget. "It used to be that this sort of thing was exciting and made life interesting, we'd scream at each

other and he'd pick up the dirty steak knife out of the sink, that's
what we'd do on the weekends, because there was nothing else to do
and it was boring otherwise, but none of that's going to happen any
more because I don't care if things are boring or not, I'm not going
to do it any more, and I don't think he can do it without me."

So they went to the tavern and met people Bridget knew from
school, and everybody asked how every one was doing. Ronnie
Beaton from her free period, who was only five-two and two hundred pounds and was working in the woods now, was drunk and
dancing with everyone. He came up to her late in the evening and
said that she was the nicest girl in school and the only girl who ever
gave him the time of day, and he would always remember her.

"That's a nice thing to say," said Bridget, astonished.

Ronnie reached over and patted her stomach.

"I hear ya had a little one." Stephen Cameron clenched on her
behalf. Bridget began to laugh and Ronnie looked confused. He was
the first person to come right out and say it, after all this time.

"I did, I did," she said, the table watching her. "I didn't keep it,
though, Ronnie."

"Oh dear Lord," said Ronnie.

"It's okay."

"I didn't know. I feel right bad." His dimpled red face went for-
lorn. Bridget couldn't stand it.

"Now, don't you feel right bad," she said. "We should dance." It
was Ronnie's favourite song, "Bad to the Bone," so he was happy to.
He flounced ahead of her, cat-hat bobbing off toward the red, flash-
ing dance-floor.

"Do you know what that was?" she announced to everyone when
she sat down. "That was what you call the maternal instinct kicking
in, me byes."

Troy Bezanson started trying to knock the hat off Daniel Sutherland
near the end of the night, so they decided they might as well go
home since last call had come and gone anyhow. Troy Bezanson

yelled that Daniel was a pussy as they rose from the table. And then for some reason he yelled, "Goodnight, Bridget, bye-bye, Bridget, you have fun now." Sing-song and laughing.

"We were lucky," said Stephen outside, waiting for Heidi to finish throwing up in the snow bank.

"I've always been lucky," said Bridget, who was getting funnier and funnier.

Walking home was a fog, but it seemed to Bridget that she fell into several snow banks and each time had the feeling she'd like to stay there, but Dan Sutherland pulled her out again. She tried to explain to him how soft they were, made of fine, white powder and not ice-made, wet flakes as usual. It was hardly even cold. I know, I know, he kept saying. Stephen had taken Heidi home. The snow had stopped blowing around and the night was clear. Dan kept telling her that he was nineteen years old, and it was only natural for a nineteen-year-old male to want to get laid all the time no matter who he happens to be with, and it was nothing to feel guilty about. Stephen told him he should think about other people, he said, but for the most part he only thought about himself and he thought he was lucky to have that ability, that it wasn't as bad as it sounded. Bridget made some joke about how, if a fella wanted to get laid, she was probably a good bet. And Bridget remembered that they kept telling jokes the whole time and laughing their heads off, laughing like crazy, but she could hardly remember any of them the next day. The next day she felt as if she had committed murder or something. And she was sick because she had eaten so much.

Everybody had been in bed and all the lights were off except for the Christmas tree and the kitchen stove, so it felt very cozy after being out in the snow. And there was a plate of squares covered with Saran Wrap that her mother had made. They had white frosting, and her mother had done this thing with green and red candied cherries to make a little holly decoration on every one. They struck Bridget as fantastically appetizing all of a sudden. She unwrapped them and ate a couple, and suddenly she was so hungry she could think about nothing else.

The good thing was all the leftovers in the fridge. She took out turkey and stuffing and potatoes and congealed gravy and cranberry sauce and got some biscuits and sat at the table making little sandwiches for herself, dipping them in the gravy. She must have eaten a million little sandwiches. And she kept thinking to herself: These are Christmas dinner sandwiches. You have a whole Christmas dinner in one sandwich. Each sandwich is just a bite of Christmas dinner. You could make a bunch of these and bring them to the church teas and bake sales and whatnot and everyone would love them.

The bad thing was that she had to put all the stuff back when she was done, and she was so full and tired she only wanted to sleep. And then she dropped the bowl of potatoes and had to pick them all up and put them in the garbage, and all of this woke Margaret P., who started pounding on the wall with, it sounded like, her Kleenex box. So Bridget knew she would have to go in to quiet her before the whole house was up.

"Who's that?"

"Bridget."

"I thought I smelled ye."

Bridget noticed that Margaret P. had been talking like a Robert Burns poem for the past couple of months. Bernadette said it was regression because Margaret P. had been born in Scotland. Bernadette said that when people reach Margaret P.'s age, they can remember details from their own childhoods as clear as day but can't tell you what happened five minutes ago.

Margaret P. was reaching out her hand, so Bridget sat down beside her and held it. Margaret P.'s hand was unpleasant to look at, full of blue and red veins you could see quite clearly, as though her skin, except for the old-lady blotches, was as transparent as the Saran Wrap over Joan's squares. It felt weak and dry.

"What is it, there, Gramma?"

"Och. Sit with me."

"What can I do for you?"

"Just sit here. I don't want to die alone."

"You're not dying yet."

"Where's Peter Joseph Pat?"

"Grampa died a while back, dear," said Bridget, unconsciously adopting the tone her mother and Bernadette always took with Margaret P.

"Ach. I know he's dead. I just thought you might know where he is."

"I imagine he's in heaven," Bridget said, looking around. She remembered that Margaret P.'s room used to scare her. She had pictures of Christ on the cross and the Virgin Mary hanging up everywhere. And little statues of Mary with her chest open like someone having heart surgery, her heart hanging out and dripping blood. Glowing. Even the Virgin's heart had a halo around it, even as it bled. Bridget never understood the bleeding heart thing. She didn't think it was in the Bible anywhere. Her grandmother even had this 3D plaque that was nothing but a bleeding heart, you couldn't tell if it was Christ's or Mary's, it was just a bleeding heart with thorns around it, all on its own. That's what used to scare her. And Margaret P. had these pictures that you could plug in at night, and if you looked at them from different angles the picture would change. The one above her bed went from Jesus, grown-up, looking skyward, to Mary and the baby. Mary looking down at the baby. Bridget used to watch it, moving her head slowly back and forth to see the picture change. It used to be that you could get *Star Wars* cards out of cereal boxes that did the same thing.

Margaret P. held Bridget's hand and moaned and sighed minutely until Bridget asked what was wrong. Margaret P. repeated that she was dying and she didn't want to die alone.

"I've been shot," she remarked. "Dead from getting shot."

"You were never shot, Gramma."

"Shot in the war."

"That wasn't you." Who was it? Bridget racked her brain. Who did Margaret P. know who was shot in the war? Her brother?

"That was your brother," she ventured.

"Ach! My brother was no shot in the war! It was cousin Hugh."

"Well, it wasn't you, in any event."

"Yes, it *was* Hugh."

"It wasn't *you* though, Gramma, *you* weren't shot in the war, you're right here with *me*!"

Margaret P. looked offended and turned to the wall, whispering prayers, and Bridget thought she would fall asleep right where she was sitting. Margaret P. began to make weeping noises.

"Why are you crying?"

"I'm praying."

"No, you were praying, but now you're crying."

"Oh," said Margaret P. "Ooooooooh! Will nobody give me the bedpan?" This was probably what she had wanted in the first place.

Bridget gave her the bedpan. It was always a trying thing, you had to lift the covers and help Margaret P. raise herself up and position her old arse just so on top of it. Bridget thought it must be uncomfortable for her to do it like that, but it was probably easier than sitting up would be. Bridget had never liked this. She thought, This was what Bernadette did every day, this sort of thing Bernadette had made a career of. Gabby too.

Margaret P. made irritated noises and Bridget smelled that she had shat. She would have to dump the thing, now, and rinse it out with some bleach. This is what it was, she remembered, this was what made her like music so much, this was what sent her to her room to listen to loud, loud music, this was what had her calling Mark at three in the morning asking him to meet her, this was why she put up with Chantal and the stuffed animals, telling stories of the girls she had tortured. Happily, Bridget did it happily, thinking she was making herself free. Drinking and doing hot knives and puking, always puking, and waking up in the mornings with one eye pointing off in the wrong direction and no feeling in the skin surrounding it. It was all coming back. It had been selfishness, it had all been selfishness. Wanting to be herself, wanting to be alone. That was selfish. You can't be that way when there is an old woman and her retarded son to look after.

Bridget did penance. She dumped and rinsed the bedpan and put a clean cloth underneath Margaret P.'s arse to replace the soiled one. Margaret P. blessed Bridget before she left the room, making the sign of the cross at her like a priest would.

She threw up all the little Christmas dinner sandwiches and her father was going around saying she was back to her ways.

"Back to her ways, back to her ways. I can Jesus friggin bastard see it now. Right back on the proverbial fucking horse she gets, never learning a goddamned Jesus bastard thing."

"I just ate too much," said Bridget. "I was really hungry when I got home."

"Too sick to come downstairs with her family but as soon as the friends call, out the door, eating and drinking up a storm."

Everybody made a big thing out of it. They wanted to call Solomon but Solomon would be on holidays.

"There's no need to bother her anyways," said Bridget.

"Well, obviously nothing has changed."

"What was supposed to change?" Bridget lay on the couch in the living room all day, everyone coming in and out to talk to her, and then going back into the kitchen to confer. Her father kept talking about the nuns. He had wanted her to go and live with the nuns in the first place, but had anybody listened to him? Oh no. He guessed he was nothing but comic relief around this whore of a place. Not a word taken seriously.

"It's my fault," she heard Albert say. "Setting the bad example."

"No, no, no, Albert," said Joan.

"That's exactly right," said Robert. "You sure as Jesus haven't helped flitting around here all through the holidays like a fat, drunken sugar plum fairy. Who wants a snort? Who wants a snort? — all hours of the day."

"We'll take her back up with us," said Albert, anguished. "I'll take her to the AA with me."

"No, you won't be taking her to any goddamn smoke-filled festival of arse-hole losers while I'm drawing breath. All you bastards do is talk about how much you enjoyed it until you can't stand it any more and fall right back off the wagon again."

"We'll do the buddy system," said Albert.

"Buddy me hole."

Albert shuffled into the living room and looked at her with sober, dewy eyes. "Would you like to come back to the city with me and Bernadette, dear?"

"Sure," said Bridget. "I can take pottery."

"See? She wants to take the pottery," he told every one in the kitchen.

"Pottery me hole."

"Well, if that's what she'd like to do," said Joan. "Gerard, can't you talk to her?"

"No," said Gerard. "I'm just getting a biscuit."

"This is not a big deal," Bridget hollered from the couch.

"She says it's not a big deal."

"Not a big deal is right."

"Well," said Joan, sighing. "Maybe it's not."

Her father came out. "What have you got against the nuns?"

"I don't have anything against the nuns. But I don't think you can just go and live with them, can you? Anyone who feels like living with the nuns just goes and lives with them. I mean, I would think that you have to want to be a nun."

"Well, maybe that's something to think about," he said, heading back to the conference.

Bridget smiled at the ceiling, but then thought that maybe it was something to think about after all. Mark had gone to live with the monks for a while and said it was wonderful. But she didn't think nuns would be the same as monks. You always saw nuns on the street doing things, teaching school and visiting the sick and what-not. The children's hospital had been full of nuns. You never saw monks anywhere doing anything. And a nun had come to see her when she was in the adult hospital, too. She said she was just mak-ing rounds, that she tried to visit all the patients. Bridget had ignored the nun, so the nun started talking to Bridget's roommate, a woman who had been six months pregnant but had to have it terminated because there was something wrong. And as the nun spoke with her, the woman began really crying, and the nun pulled the curtain over, murmuring. Thanks a lot, nun, Bridget had thought then. She was fine until you came along.

"We have to figure out what you're going to do," Joan said, bringing her tea. Joan sat the tray down on the coffee table and balanced her small behind on the edge of the couch beside her. "You're eighteen."

"The world is my oyster."

"You could do anything, really."

"Like what."

"Your dad and I were thinking you could take a secretarial course at the vocational school. Or else he could probably phone up Leland MacPhedron . . . get you on at the Busy Burger."

"Isn't that closing down?"

"They're just doing renovations."

"I thought Leland was being indicted for something."

"Well — that shouldn't affect his business too much. His boys pretty much run the place now anyway."

Oh, God. That would mean she would have to work for Duncan MacPhedron, whom she had rolled around in the mud with down at the trails when she was fifteen after splitting a bottle of Great White. Bridget looked at the ceiling, humming. It made her feel less hung over when she hummed. She had an unpleasant memory. She had hummed after procreating. She hadn't been able to help it. Her body was shaking convulsively, and she kept humming. Then she would force herself to stop, remind herself that this was the worst thing there was, and then she'd start humming again. "What are you doing?" her mother had asked her, and she'd sputtered laughter. "I have to hum!" Joan looked at the nurses, worried, worried. "What's she doing? Why is she shaking like that?"

"It's the experience," the nurse said, and spread a heated sheet over Bridget. Bridget hadn't known about the heated sheets. The heated sheet was wonderful. And when it cooled off, they spread another one over the first one.

Bridget remembered her mother repeating to herself, "The Experience. It's The Experience," talking to herself like Rollie — probably because her mother had never had The Experience and saw now that it entailed things she'd never imagined, that her own mother hadn't told her, things you didn't hear about on TV or in books. Like shaking and humming and pulling the heated sheet up over your face and saying "I'm sorry," guilty as the first woman. Bridget wondered if her mother had been prepared for the fact that people pooed when they procreated. Because Bridget hadn't been. She remembered the sound of a hard pellet dropping into a waiting metal bedpan and being in between contractions and just clear-headed enough to feel ashamed.

Bridget stopped humming because her mother was looking at her as if she were reminded of everything as well. Her mother looked sorrowful, despairing, which was hard to look at because her mother constantly worked so hard to feel otherwise, for everybody to.

"I try to make things nice," she said.

"Oh God, Mumma."

"I want everyone to be happy."

"Don't."

"Don't you do this anymore?" Cry, she meant.

"Don't, Mumma."

"I'm not trying to make you feel bad."

"No."

"It just seems like everything is an uphill battle."

"Yes, well."

"Don't you even think about him?"

"What?"

"Don't you even think about him?"

"No," said Bridget, rising to vomit.

"I can't stay if it's going to be like this," Bridget said when she returned from the bathroom. She knew what they wanted most was for her to stay. None of their ideas about what she should do with her life involved her leaving. Except for going to live with the nuns, which wasn't really leaving at all.

"I can't stay if I have to feel like this." She knew she sounded very calm and rational. She was able to do this now, and her father and Gerard didn't like it. Gerard used to be able to tease her into tears and her father only had to raise his voice. Bridget's parents had told her that she used to cower, when she was a baby, whenever she heard her father's rifle-shot voice. They thought she was a timid baby. They thought maybe it had something to do with being adopted. They thought that about most things for the first few years of her life. How she sucked her thumb all the time. How, when Joan tried to toilet train her, she would climb into the bathtub, pull the curtain over and go in her drawers, singing "Oh Dear Me."

"Where would you go, now, ya figure?" her father called from the kitchen, where every one had gone into slow motion, and Rollie's fiddle music on the radio had been turned down. Her father tried to make a snorting noise. She heard Rollie mutter:

"Hal-fax. Hal-fax by the Lor' Jes' Chris' Almi'hy. Where Bri-het goin'?"

"I'm eighteen," called Bridget.

Stephen Cameron wanted her to go to the Dairy Queen after supper. Nobody liked that she was going out again. They felt that it was not the right thing for her to do after upsetting them so much. Again the notion of being properly penitent seemed to be lost on Bridget. Bridget was feeling the pressure of this expectation all the time. It was getting so that she wanted to be out of the house again. When Stephen Cameron asked her to go to the Dairy Queen, she jumped at the chance. They also didn't like that she was going to meet a guy, Stephen, which was funny. Stephen was physically fish-like to Bridget. Grey in complexion, open-mouthed. Something of a sheen to him.

She regretted it as soon as they were sitting across from one another with their one-dollar sundaes. Stephen had eaten a whole Full-meal-deal and said he would buy her one too if she wanted, but she had no appetite and was surprised to see Stephen eating so much after the night before.

"Electrolytes," Stephen had said, eating french fries. But Stephen was always eating trash. You could not walk down the street with him for five minutes without having to stop into a convenience store for pop and chips and a bar. He bought the same three items all time, never just pop, or just chips, or just a bar. Or never just pop and chips. It was always pop and chips (ketchup) and a bar (Big Turk). It never mattered what kind of pop, as long as it was cola. He seemed to think all three went together. He had acne all through school.

So Stephen ate and bought her a sundae and got down to business, arranging his face into his own particular expression of cynical concern. It tried to say, yes, we can all agree that the world's a piece of shit, but there is one situation, at least, that I am in the middle of, that only I can rectify, and damned if I won't do it.

"I'm sorry about last night," he said.

"Why? I had a good time."

"I'm sorry if Dan was bugging ya."

"Dan's nice, I like Dan."

Stephen began stabbing the centre of his sundae with the plastic spoon. "I just thought it would be good for you to get out, have some fun." This reminded Bridget of a few years ago when her mother would take Margaret P. out to play Bingo. The sentiment seemed the same.

"I just wanted to be a friend," Stephen whispered.

His eyes were moist and grey with sincerity, and Bridget was aware that he was trying to lead up to something big and melodramatic and she didn't want to encourage it. It used to be, in high school, that she would have encouraged it. Like every body else, she would have been overjoyed to see a melodrama on the horizon. Something to do. Something to talk about. A crisis with which to occupy your thoughts. People were still using her for that, she guessed. Jennifer MacDonnell was on the opposite side of the sky, fading.

"What do you hear of Archie Shearer?" Bridget asked, to test her theory.

Stephen blinked at her, fish-mouthed. "What? He's guilty. He's going to jail." Stephen flicked his fingers as if he had blown his nose on them.

That was that. That was the story of Archie Shearer and Jennifer MacDonnell. The top of Jennifer MacDonnell's orange head, disappearing into the water on the other side of the causeway.

CHAPTER 13

He wanted to tell her that Mark was cross to hear she had been to the tavern. He called up Stephen that afternoon, all pissed off, because he thought Stephen was his friend. Stephen said he felt trapped in the middle of things and didn't know what to do. Bridget listened to him talk, not responding, because she wanted to show him that he wasn't in the middle of anything at all, that there was nothing on either side of him. Stephen said he loved his friends more than anything, his family didn't mean shit to him, but without friends what do you have? So he wanted things to be good for everyone. He tried to tell Mark that he just wanted to be supportive. But Mark had heard about her and Dan Sutherland.

"Nothing me and Dan Sutherland," Bridget said.

"Well, you guys *were* sorta fucking around that night," Stephen reproached, smiling like an understanding grandparent. Confess, confess, so we can get on with this game, he was saying.

Bridget watched him poking at his ice cream, looking quickly up at her and then down at the ice cream again. I have to get out of here, she thought, lucid. She knew that to say something like "He only walked me home," or "Nothing happened," or anything, any sort of acknowledgement, would be taking part. And she knew she did not want to be taking part in things any more, that was the one certainty she had taken away from the whole ordeal. The one course of action she felt was right.

Stephen was waiting for her to say something. He waited and

waited. His ice cream was chocolate slush. Finally he sighed and shook his head, smiling with affection at her.

"He said you could be like this."

"I have to go," Bridget said, looking around. For some reason the situation was wholly unnerving, even though Stephen had to be the most unintimidating male she knew with his white, weak hands, an eye-of-the-tiger ring on the right one. George and Chantal walked into the restaurant then, Chantal with her parka open and the four gold chains George had given her spanning her tiny throat. Bridget remembered that they hung out there all the time. Chantal liked the Brownie Delights. All of them had hung out there all the time, she remembered. Stephen knew this, but she'd forgotten. It was as if Bridget was only now remembering where she was, that she was home, that she was in the place that had seemed, for the months on the ward, like one long, lurid movie she had watched eons ago whose plot she could no longer remember.

Stephen saw George and Chantal and decided that was why she wanted to leave. He nodded to her and actually winked, gesturing toward the door with his head. Bridget was surprised he didn't put his finger to his nose. As they were dumping their trays into the garbage, Chantal said something. Some loud comment, ostensibly to George. She repeated it as they reached the door, but Bridget couldn't hear it. She thought everything was ridiculous. Outside, making their way through a powdery snow bank, Stephen tried to take her by the arm. He imagined she must be weak with guilt and grief and horror.

"I'm going to do everything I can," he kept saying to her.

She was going to call Alan Voorland. He had written her a few weeks back, an endless letter on four pages of graph paper, his writing infinitesimal. In the letter he said what he thought about her and the things she must be going through, and he said what he thought would happen to her in the future. He listed off the things she should and should not do with her life and said for her to please write to him often, to please keep in touch, because he cared about her and she could always talk to him. They had something special.

Then Alan talked about his life now that he was home in Guelph, how good it had been to call up all his old friends, how his parents threw a "welcome home" party for him. He and his girlfriend had been skiing up a storm throughout the holidays, were talking about moving to Hamilton together, where he could surely get a job after his experience at the mill. Christmas, he said, was "magical." Alan said that his father had given him his car as a pre-Christmas present because he wanted to buy a new one.

So Bridget called him. Everything sounded great where Alan was. His mother answered the phone, amazingly pleasant-voiced, calling to him sweetly.

"Oh God," said Alan. "I will call you back in ten minutes."

"I wanted to come into the den. I was right in the middle of all this family shit. Hey! How are you!"

"Good, good. Kinda boring down here. How are you?"

"I've been meaning to call you, actually," his voice going low and serious. He blew out a breath, causing static in Bridget's ear. "Things have been pretty tense around here lately."

"Oh, yeah?"

"It's hard to talk about," he said. "But I've been dying to talk to you about it."

"What's wrong?"

"Well," said Alan, blowing more static into Bridget's ear. "A couple of weeks before Christmas, Deanna and I realized we were pregnant."

"Oh, no."

"Yeah. Not good. I mean it must've happened *the* night I got home. Sort of put a damper on the whole homecoming, if you know what I mean."

"It's pretty early."

"Yeah, but she knows. You must know what that's like. Knowing."

"No."

"Well, it completely took me aback, after this whole thing with meeting you."

"I can imagine."

"You must have rubbed some of your fertility dust on me or something, bitch," he laughed. Bridget laughed. "Well," he said at last. "It looks like we're going to have to have an abortion."

"I would think so . . ."

"What do you mean you think so? You of all people should know that there's other alternatives."

Bridget opened her mouth thinking she would say: Yes, but real human beings shouldn't have to go through that.

"But, no, you're right, of course. Deanna doesn't want a baby. I don't want a baby. But it's. Man. It's hard once you start thinking about it."

"Don't think about it."

"That's your advice, is it?" She could hear him smiling.

"The best I know."

"The appointment is made and everything. We have to wait a few more weeks. It's been hard on Deanna."

"Yeah . . ."

"I'm going to go with her, of course. I'm going to be with her every step of the way."

"That's good a ya."

"I've been thinking I should keep a journal of my thoughts throughout the whole . . . ordeal. Keep track of everything."

"Why?"

"Why? Well, you don't have an abortion every day, do you? I want to remember how it feels. That is, maybe it'll help me . . . come to grips with how I feel."

For some reason, how Alan said "come to grips" repelled Bridget. Alan had been talking from his diaphragm the entire time. His announcer's voice.

"In the end," said Alan "this will probably be good for me. I mean, I'll probably learn from this experience and grow as a result."

What foolishness it was. What foolishness to think that any good could come at all. As if it were some sort of cosmic therapy, sent by God.

Bridget thought she would enjoy hearing Alan talk, like she used to. As it was, he talked on and on about his feelings, about how this would affect his relationship with his girlfriend, and she listened like she always did. Only after he told her to write him a big letter, wished her goodbye and hung up, Bridget remembered what she had wanted to say in the first place. That she didn't know what to do with herself and did he think he could help her?

Bridget fantasized that Mona would call and ask her to go to Florida. She would take all that money and buy Bridget a plane ticket to Ontario, and from there they would drive the whole way. Mona once said that when she was in Florida and her father had reported his credit cards stolen, she had to work as a stripper for a while. She said this one man who came in to see her all the time would always offer her wads of money to come to his house and take a crap on him. Strip joints are full of freaks, Mona told Bridget, don't let any one tell you different. Don't ever let anybody tell you it's just good wholesome fun, that's what everybody told me and that's why I did it. She laughed her head off, telling this story, but then her pink face got very still, and she said she hoped Bridget didn't think less of her. It was not that Bridget thought less of her but that she didn't quite believe Mona at the time. She thought it was possible that Mona was on the ward because she was a pathological liar. After a while, though, she came to see they were all true, all of Mona's stories. They were funny and appalling, like real life.

Bridget thought that if she went to Florida, she could sit on the beach and make snowflakes, selling them to passers-by. She thought people in Florida were sure to be enchanted by them. And maybe she would stuff a suitcase full of her father's ducks and sell them, too. And maybe she would take a bunch of Rollie's religious statues and sell them, holding a Bible against herself. And maybe she would rant at the passers-by, quoting scripture at them.

When she was little, she thought she would do something like that. She thought she would wander the earth like John the Baptist, hollering the truth at people. She had seen some religious movie at Easter time about John the Baptist, and the actor playing him had looked like a crazed caveman and everyone was afraid of him, and for some reason that had appealed to Bridget.

As grandiose as it was, mostly she had wanted to be Jesus. A religion teacher had told her that Jesus was perfect, and the more perfect Bridget was the more like Jesus she would be. So Bridget had walked around trying to be perfect for a while. It was a recipe for madness, she supposed.

When the nice priest found her hiding in the woods by herself, among the discarded chunks of concrete — the presence of which she never understood — the priest had taken her into his house and called her parents and put on Beethoven's Opus 95 for her (she remembered this detail ridiculously), and when she told him about eating the licorice and feeling that she would never be Jesus, the priest told her that she shouldn't worry, that she could do no wrong in the eyes of Jesus because she was a child, and Jesus said "Suffer the little children to come unto me." Did Bridget know what that meant? It meant that Jesus *liked* little boys and girls, and little boys and girls make a lot of mistakes and Jesus understood that. He told her that Jesus forgave her everything as long as she was truly sorry, which Bridget obviously was, full of grass and dirt.

This made her feel better, but ultimately the priest's solicitude had failed. Because once Bridget hit fourteen, saw the lumps pushing their way up under her shirt, started getting all the stuff at school, the movies and the pamphlets, started cramping and bleeding, began to witness her parents' horror, Gerard's disgust, she knew she had left the state of grace and could get away with nothing any more.

"I would become a nun," Bridget said at the dinner table on New Year's Eve, "except I don't think there would be any point now." This ended the discourse on Bridget living with nuns.

Albert and Bernadette had gone. There was talk about her going up with them, but it was too late to apply for school, so they thought they would leave it for the time being. Gerard had gone with them. His school didn't start for another week, but he wanted to start studying for exams. Albert hugged her and tried to be brusque. This was another anomaly she noticed in Albert that made him unlike anybody else. While everyone else attempted to make ersatz gestures of love and solicitation, Albert had to pretend to be the crusty old woodsman he saw himself as. He had to cough and say his eyes were red and sore from the hangover. He told her not to bother with the drinking any more. He kept saying it would come to naught.

"She comes to naught, my dear one, she comes to naught, all that there business. What the hell, maybe twice in your life you have yourself a whore of a good time, and then you spend every night of the rest of your life trying to get that good time back. But she comes to naught." Bridget's father stood by with his arms folded. "Robert," said Albert, his eyes brightening, thinking of the good times, "do you remember the time we stuck JimmyArchie Gillis on the ferry to Newfoundland the night of his wedding? Nothing on him but a pair of hip waders?"

Now Albert was gone. She thought if she had been a boy it would have been more fun. She would have got to go hunting with Albert and her father and Albert's five sons. Gerard had never liked to go because Albert's boys would pick on him because he didn't like the blood, didn't like having to castrate the bucks the moment after they killed them. But Bridget would have gone, if she had been a boy. She would have killed and castrated the deer and gutted them on the spot. She would have sat around the campfire with the boys, passing around a thermos of hot buttered rum. Gerard told her about this, how Albert's sons would talk about life in the army, life fishing, life as an electrician. Albert's sons were all very much alike, were best friends with one another, and would sit telling the same stories over and over again for the amusement of the other ones. "Pod-people" Gerard called Albert's sons. He thought they were losers. They had chased him around the forest with a deer intestine.

She thought all that would have been more fun. All she could remember doing was watching TV and drinking at the trails. Sitting among stuffed animals listening to Chantal talk about all the different forms of birth control she had tried, or sitting with Heidi talking about things like proms. Proms. And up until recently, drinking with Mark, offending Mark. Mark getting cross with her and she getting cross with Mark. Figuring they were the next Sid and Nancy. Someone storming out of the party, someone else following them. Someone throwing a fit in the kitchen, someone staying to talk to them. Monday morning at school they would make up until the next weekend. Bridget saw it now as foolishness and a terrible waste. She thought it would have been more fun to fish the Margarees with Albert's lot, like they did every weekend of the summer.

They took her out the one time, on the ocean, to go deep sea fishing. They gave her a hook and told her to jig it up and down. Everyone stood at the sides of the boat doing this. Her father had thrown up in the little boat-bathroom and not told any one, but it was impossible to hide it.

Bridget was sure she would never get a fish because all of Albert's sons were there. But she got five fish. The first time she saw the cod's big face coming towards her from the depths of the ocean, she screamed, she was so excited, hollering, "What do I do? What do I do now?" and the captain of the boat had taken it from her swiftly and filleted the thing before she could even get her hook back in the water. And all the boys whooped and slapped her on the back because she had caught the first fish. And four more fish faces, with their horrified mouths, came at her from the bottom of the sea, and Albert's boys whooped on her behalf every time.

That had been the best day. She was cold and wet when she got home, her three sweaters soaked through, because it had rained on their way back to land. They took pictures of Bridget with her biggest catch. Her hair had been stringy, in her face because she was bending with the weight of the fish.

Bridget felt she should have been doing this sort of thing all along.

The moment they left, her father went to the tree and started pulling the balls and the garlands from it. "You get your arse over here and help me with this," he said to her. "I hate this part." One of the garlands was stuck, tangled up in a branch, and he fought with it.

"Happy New Year," he had said into the phone at midnight. "Jennifer MacDonnell rots in the earth."

CHAPTER 14

Young Jenny Mac was seventeen
When she was laid to bed,
Young Jenny Mac will ne'er grow old
Nor will she ever wed.

A sweeter girl you never saw,
Her parent's special pride,
She had a smile for all she knew
Until the day she died

It went on like that. A fiddler from West Bay wrote it, apparently a relative of the MacDonnells. It was long and mournful, they played it on the radio all day long. It went on and on, actually going into lurid detail about Jenny meeting Archie and Archie chasing her with a gun and pointing it in her face and saying:

If you'll not be my love,
You'll be the love of none.

And then it had Jennifer going:

O, Archie if you ever loved
The kisses these lips gave,
Then listen now to what they say,
Don't send me to my grave.

Bridget thought it sounded an awful lot like "The Wild Colonial Boy," but her mother turned it up whenever it came on and always took up a handful of Kleenex. Bridget's mother said "The Wild Co-

lonial Boy" was about a real person, too, but to Bridget, that wasn't
the point. The song *sounded* the same. Nobody cared about that,
however.

The MacDonnells, apparently, were much soothed by this song.
Heidi said that she and her parents had been to see them, and their
living room was like a shrine to the girl. They had a light shining on
her prom picture in which she wore a puffy white gown and looked
like a fairy. And a CD with the single "The Ballad of Jenny Mac" on
it that the fiddler had autographed and dedicated to them. Heidi
and her mother thought it was beautiful and cried with Mrs.
MacDonnell. But Heidi said Mr. MacDonnell had stayed in his
room the whole time. Heidi and her mother were the sort of mother
and daughter who could do that sort of thing, they could go and
visit virtually anyone in town, at the worst moments of their lives,
bearing a plate of date squares or the like. And the families would
always take Heidi and her mother into their homes and cry and
share their grief and be grateful to the two of them. This sort of
thing was entirely foreign to Bridget. She remembered when Peter
Joseph Pat had died, they did the same thing, going directly to the
relatives who really cared about Peter Joseph Pat, like Albert and his
kids, who were older than Bridget and Gerard and remembered Peter
Joseph Pat when he was fun and could do things with them. Heidi
had only come to talk to Bridget once she had paid her respects to
those who were truly bereaved. Bridget rather admired this ability of
Heidi's. She was one of those people who knew, instinctively, how to
be good in such situations. It was like a ritual her mother had passed
down to her. Wait a few days. Pay a discreet visit. Bring an offering
of food. Speak in short, supportive sentences, in gentle tones.

And after all that, Heidi would sidle up to Bridget, punch her in
the arm and say, "Where's all the booze around here? Want me to
grab you a sandwich?"

Bridget saw that there was an etiquette where death was concerned. Just like everything else. And Jennifer MacDonnell, who had
never been called Jenny in her life, had sunk entirely beneath the

horizon. Something else being erected in her place. She was queen of the prom, on her parent's mantelpiece forever, now.

They were calling her up all the time to go out and she couldn't fathom why. Bridget didn't suppose she was a lot of fun. Heidi and Stephen. They were something of an item now, strangely. Although Heidi had always been rather popular, she always went after the strangest boys. Boys who were not popular or unpopular but simply peripheral. Who were a little too skinny or whose heads were slightly too large. Finally she had come around to Stephen, and Stephen was trying to be cool about it.

She laughed about him on the phone, about his serious ways. He always got weepy about Bridget, she said. Bridget and Mark. He hated to see them so unhappy.

"Who's unhappy?"

"Not you? Then why don't you ever come out?"

"I dunno."

"You're afraid you're gonna see him."

"That's not it."

"You shouldn't be. Steve figures if you two could just get together and talk things over, it'd all work out."

"No. No. He hates me anyways." It was a mistake for her to have added the last part.

"No! That's not true! He's just upset about all that's happened."

"Oh, shit, I don't care, I don't care, Heidi."

"Why do you think he hates you?"

"It doesn't matter."

"But why?"

"He calls every once in a while to say so."

"Look," said Heidi. "He feels bad about that."

"How do you know?"

"We see him."

"We?"

"Me and Steve." Heidi was always calling Stephen "Steve" now that they were a thing. "We all got drunk a couple of times."

Bridget realized she was in it. She was in it just because she was talking to Heidi on the phone. She hadn't thought it could do any harm, but she was in it. They make you be in it. Heidi was inexorable.

"We're just about to have supper," Bridget told her.

But Heidi found her at the post office the next day. Her parents had her going across the street to get the mail every day because they thought she needed little things to do. Every time she went, there were people she knew who said they had heard she was back. Bridget was wearing a pyjama shirt under her coat, and Heidi wanted her to go for a walk to the Dairy Queen.

"No Dairy Queen," said Bridget.

"The donut place, then."

So they plowed across the field, moving in the direction opposite to Jennifer MacDonnell's when she was shot.

"Somebody said the town was going to plant a tree here in the spring or something," Heidi remarked.

Bridget looked over her shoulder at Alan Voorland's old apartment building and saw Tina the midget struggling to hold the door open while she rammed a baby-stroller through the crack, plumes of cold breath rising from her mouth. Not thinking about it, she went over to help, pushing the door open wide like Alan had done for her that one time. The door was not heavy in the least — Tina's body was just incredibly powerless.

"You got your baby back," Bridget observed.

"This here's a new one, can't you tell?"

"It looks the same as the old one."

"Not any more," said Tina. "Not that I would know. I'm lucky if I see him once a month."

"How's Christa?"

"She calls the foster mother Mum now. I'm in the rehab. They don't care. Why don't you come up for a shot?"

Bridget actually wanted to. It was a perverse longing to be with some one who was really sad, really, legitimately sad. Somebody else's overwhelming thing to wallow in for a while. Tina was infinitesimal in a second-hand pink child's parka, and it was strange to look down and see her grey hair, her lined mouth. The lines around her eyes were magnified by her crooked little glasses.

"They want me to be lonely," she said, goggling up at Bridget. "They want me to be poor and alone. Well, maybe I can't work, with the hip, but I can sure as fuck have babies. They can't stop me from having my babies." Like Christa, like the other one, Tina's new baby looked vital and healthy in a freshly bought, very bright yellow snowsuit. Its blue eyes were clear and alert, and it regarded Tina with impatience. Bridget thought it would open its wet mouth soon and tell her to hurry along.

"No, they can't," agreed Bridget, picking up the stroller and carrying it up the stairs to Tina's floor. The baby screamed briefly, thinking it was being taken away as Tina clambered behind.

Heidi said Bridget was weird because of all that, and because she took off her jacket in the donut shop and sat showing her pyjamas to the world until Heidi, returning from the counter with coffees and eclairs, told her to put the jacket back on.

"You're going strange on us," she said. "Queer as me arse."

"No."

"Yes."

"I was just getting the mail. I didn't think I'd be going anywhere."

For some reason, Heidi started to sing "There's a Tear in my Beer," drumming her fingers on the table. Bridget waited for her to finish. "That's not what I meant," she said finally. "I don't see why you don't come out."

"I'm out now."

"Out drinking, stupid-arse!"

"I've been drinking at home."

"Oh, that's healthy, now. Social drinking, stupid-arse."

"Not so healthy getting shit-faced and passing out in a snow bank."

"Getting all puritanical."

Bridget said nothing. Let Heidi think she was getting all puritanical. But Heidi didn't really think that.

"Stephen thinks I should talk to you."

"I know. I know. I know what Stephen thinks."

"Well?"

"He's wrong and I don't want to."

Heidi looked relieved. She didn't really want to either.

"I just want us all to have fun like we used to."

But Bridget couldn't remember having fun. Heidi looked at her, chagrined, annoyed. Maybe insulted because she could see that.

"We had fun that night we all went out," she protested. "Boxing Day."

"Sure we did."

"Well, why can't we do that again?"

"It was a special occasion," Bridget answered lamely. She couldn't answer anything that was the truth. That it was no fun, that there was no point, that she would have preferred to be deep sea fishing, that she only did it thinking Heidi would leave her alone afterwards, which had been naive. Bridget took a large drink of coffee, forgetting what it was, and burned her entire mouth. Heidi threw up her hands and said she was hopeless.

"Right you are," said Bridget. Wanting that to be the end of it.

It was only a matter of time, though, before Heidi thought to get some booze into her. They went to Heidi's house and sat at the table with her mother, drinking up the homemade Irish creme and listening to "The Ballad of Jenny Mac" on the stereo. Heidi's family still had their Christmas lights up in the windows, and so the three of them sat in the flickering red and green, feeling festive, as if the holiday hadn't already come and gone. Heidi and her mother talked to one another like sisters, and soon Heidi's father came up from the rec room to "see what all the commotion was about." Heidi's family was always eerily at ease with one another, Heidi saying things like "stuff it up yer hole" to her father, and the three of them laughing about the time she came home at three in the morning with her sweater turned inside out.

Heidi's parents were nice to Bridget, saying they always thought she was a lovely girl, if only she would smile every so often. Heidi's father said he remembered Bridget narrating the grade three Christmas pageant, "Standing up there all straight and serious. The only one with any friggin dignity, all those boys in their bathrobes, with the hockey sticks covered in the tin foil. Why is it always the hockey sticks and tin foil? I never read anything in the Bible about hockey sticks and tin foil, did you?" He pretended to be angry about it, trying to make her laugh.

Heidi's father made them rum and Cokes when the Irish creme was gone and asked what they were up to that night, and Bridget remembered it was Friday.

"House party," Heidi answered promptly. Heidi could just tell her parents these things and they wouldn't care.

"Is that at the Sutherland boy's again?"

"Where else? Might as well get them in before he heads back up to Dal."

"I wonder if his parents know what goes on there every weekend of the year, now?"

"Why don't you call and tell them?"

"No, I think I'll just wait until you two head out and then I can call the Mounties on ya."

"I'm in my pyjamas," Bridget interjected.

"Why you old whore!" Heidi hollered at her mother, dragging Bridget into her room for a make-over. Which really meant giving her a shirt and some makeup to wear.

The bottom line was that Bridget had no bra. Heidi's didn't fit, and she didn't want to go home to get one. Bridget was not the sort of person who could go without a bra any more. But there she was, braless. Heidi gave her a bulky sweater but it didn't make much difference. Every one would still see that Bridget Murphy had no bra. Did you see Bridget Murphy at Sutherland's Friday night? Walking around with no bra. It was quite the thing, but I suppose it's her own business, if that's the way she wants to go.

"You can't even notice," Heidi kept saying.

"Oh my! Bridget Murphy! No bra!" Bridget kept saying, until Heidi saw that she didn't really care one way or another, so they left.

It was a big party. Daniel called it "The See You in Hell Party" and had a large banner over the bar he had actually set up.

He said to Bridget, "Because this is hell, and I see you in it."

"Really?"

"No."

"Then what?"

"Because I don't think I'm coming back here any more."

"Are you going to live with the nuns?" asked Bridget.

"No."

"Are you going to take pottery? In Florida?"

"No."

"Well, I don't see what it is you're going to do, then," she said.

It was one of those parties where people got drunk and holed up in clusters. People clustered together at Daniel's bar. People sat together in corners talking very seriously to each other. At one point Bridget looked up on the stairs and saw Dolores Chaisson crying and a couple of other girls talking steadily to her. There were people there whom she had never seen at Dan's parties before, like Troy Bezanson and Jason MacPherson. It was the kind of party where people you'd hardly spoken to in school came up to you and said they always liked you and wished they had known you better. Early in the evening, Bridget decided to sit on the floor beside the stereo and stay there, letting people bring her drinks. Daniel, for a joke, brought over several bottles from the bar, a glass, and a bucket of ice, and set them up in front of her. It was funny.

Stephen would sit with her and then go away for a while and then come back. Sometimes he would bring her special drinks he had made with the blender and pat her on the head.

"Whatever was the deal with that old guy, anyway?" he asked at one point.

"He's pregnant," Bridget said. "He's going to have an abortion."

Stephen gave her a look, for some reason, of loathing. He thought she was fooling with him, maybe.

Stephen was owlish because Heidi was airplaning around talking to everyone the way she always did, and Stephen didn't know how he was supposed to react. He loitered around Bridget, watching Heidi at the bar pretending to punch Troy Bezanson in the stomach.

"Are you two supposed to be going out now, or what?" Bridget asked for something to say. He turned a grotesquely sunny smile on her, entirely out of place in Dan's smoky, Pink Floyd-movie basement.

"Oh, who knows," he said. He was wearing a long black trench coat and a tie with leopard spots on it. "I suppose it's just one of those things."

Poor Stephen had never had any of those things. She didn't like him. She had the feeling suddenly that she didn't like him. How he hovered in his tie.

"I think we should call him," he started saying to her over and over again. "I know he's over at George's. I think we should call him."

"You mean Chantal's." Then Heidi flounced over.

"Heidi," said Stephen. "Don't you think we should call him?"

Heidi put her hands on her hips. "I think it's up to herself-the-elf. What does herself-the-elf think?"

Troy Bezanson came over and picked Heidi up and turned her upside down, and Stephen looked alarmed while she screamed and laughed and called him names like buttwad. Then he put Heidi down and asked Bridget if she wanted to go next. Thinking about it, Bridget realized how close to throwing up she already was.

Stephen and Heidi went off somewhere, and Troy tried to have a conversation with her. Troy Bezanson was one of the boys from school who had always unnerved Bridget. The ones with really short haircuts who boxed every weekend at the Rock-a-bye-Ross boxing club and were always together. Gerard had been something like that. Troy wanted to play caps but Bridget wasn't drinking beer. She remembered the way he had said goodbye to her at the tavern that night and thought that it hadn't seemed particularly friendly, and now he was acting another way.

But Bridget was so stupid. He probably wanted to screw her. Alan Voorland used to say to her, The sooner you realize that everyone wants to screw you the better off you'll be. And she had said something foolish and girl-like, like, No, no, I'm not even good-looking. And Alan had told her, Fuck off. You're seventeen and you're not fat. Don't kid yourself that it has anything to do with your looks or your personality or your charisma or anything about you whatsoever. It's about guys. Guys are fucking pigs and the sooner you get that figured out the better off you'll be.

Alan often talked to her like that when they drank together. He was always telling her about the things she was going to have to figure out.

I love you, he would say. I think you are glorious and beautiful and are going to get through all this and be a wonderful person, he would say. But not everybody is like me.

And he used to say to her: And another thing! Just because a guy wants to screw you doesn't necessarily mean he's going to be nice about it.

So that explained, maybe, why Troy Bezanson was an arsehole at the tavern.

Bridget was learning so much about the world.

"I see someone's performing without a net tonight," Troy said abruptly. It took Bridget a couple of minutes to figure out what he meant. While she was thinking about it, he said, "I hear you had an affair with a guy who was like forty years old."

"He's pregnant now," Bridget said. Troy laughed and laughed, rubbing her legs.

"Why are you rubbing my legs?" said Bridget.

Stephen appeared again. He wanted to know what was so funny, and Troy said that Bridget was so fertile she got men pregnant. "I guess I better look out!" he said, rubbing her legs.

"Yes, I guess you should," said Stephen. Troy stood up then, and Daniel came over at once, unfortunately wearing his bowler hat. Bridget couldn't follow their conversation for the most part, but Troy had asked Stephen, What's with the tie, anyhow, pussy? and suggested that the fact Stephen was wearing a stupid tie and Daniel was wearing a stupid hat implied that the two of them were homosexual lovers. Daniel was trying to put his arms around both of them and was telling them that since being in university he had dropped a lot of acid, and by this he meant to say that people should all love one another and get along, or some such thing.

It was strange, because then Heidi came over and defused things with a few wisecracks like she always did, and just when it looked as if Troy Bezanson was about to turn around and get another drink, his friend Jason MacPherson, who was famous for being at the donut shop when Archie Shearer killed Jennifer MacDonnell, strode up to them and punched Stephen Cameron in the face.

Stephen's glasses flew off and bounced off Bridget's head. They were fighting so close to her that she had to draw up her legs and make a ball of herself. Troy had decided to hold Stephen while Jason punched him, and so this meant that Daniel had to try and hold Jason, at which he was wholly inept. Jason MacPherson's girlfriend, some girl from Port Hood who nobody knew, was standing in the middle of the room screaming at them and crying and saying that she was going to call the fucking cops and Daniel was calling to her to please not call the cops. At one point, Stephen fell on Bridget, and all she could do was scrunch herself up some more until Jason pulled him off again. His body was unbelievably hot, noises coming out of his throat. Heidi was saying that they were all a bunch of a-holes. It only ended when some guys who had been watching saw that Stephen wasn't defending himself very satisfactorily but was just getting pummelled. There was no sport in it, so they broke it up.

Mark was never any good at fighting either, she remembered. He was small. He was small but mean, he always said, and he knew how to fight dirty. When Bridget asked if that meant kicking in the balls, he said, No, it meant being ready to pick up a chair, a glass bottle, or having a pocket knife on you at all times. Any nearby, hurtful instrument. And then waving it around like you're crazy. And you can't be afraid to use it, he always said, because otherwise you're fucked.

CHAPTER 15

She thought it had been gross, all that. Stephen bleeding on Mrs. Sutherland's kitchen floor, crying too, stuttering, saying: "F-f-f-f-f-f-ucking c-c-c-c-c-COCK!" over and over again. She recalled it with distaste.

A feeling came over Bridget at a point in the evening that she remembered from her pre-ward days. Most nights drinking, she would forget herself, forget her parents, and stay until everybody else had passed out, going around the house to sip out of abandoned glasses. But there were other evenings when that didn't happen, when something would click in her head and she'd have the perfectly clear realization that she didn't want to be there any more, that she hadn't wanted to be there in the first place, that she'd drunk enough and could go home. So she slipped out while everyone huddled around bleeding Stephen. It took her a while to find her boots. Daniel always hid her boots when she came over. One was in the fireplace and the other was in the washing machine, but she found them fairly quickly. She thought she wouldn't have found them as fast if she hadn't been drunk. There was a quality about being drunk that made things like finding your boots easier than usual. Because Mark was right when he said that God watched over drunks and small children, perhaps.

Walking up Daniel's street, large, wet flakes splatting against her face and jacket, her boobs feeling weirdly unencumbered underneath — like water balloons, like bags of water, which was probably

173

what they were, more or less — Bridget thought about God and
Christa, Tina the midget's daughter, who went tumbling through
the air in her angelic nightie, sunshine glancing off her ridiculous
blonde curls. Thinking, probably, something simplistic and child-
like, like, Uh-oh. Looking up at the retreating open window and
thinking this would get her in trouble.

Bridget saw Mark and George Matheson coming toward her
through the splattering snow, walking under a lamppost, casting
long shadows on the wet street ahead of them. It was Mark and
George, small Mark and bigger George, who wore his leather jacket
with the Harley Davidson pins all year round, no matter how hot or
how cold, and Bridget turned down a side street. She could hear
them singing "Hashe fo-um fo-um fo-um, rise and follow Charlie,"
loud and silly in overdone Scottish accents.

Heidi said later that this was when things got interesting at Dan's
house. Stephen called him just before getting pummelled, called him
and returned to find Troy Bezanson rubbing braless Bridget Murphy's
legs. The outrage of it all. Mark and George arrived to see everyone
sopping up Stephen's blood, and Stephen told them all about it.
Everyone wondered where Bridget had gone. Then Mark and
George decided they were going to go out and find Troy and Jason,
and they picked up a couple of empty J.D. bottles to take with
them. Then they said Daniel should come with them, but Daniel
said he couldn't leave with all the people in his house, and Mark,
according to Heidi, suddenly got mad and told Daniel he was a
fucking pussy who didn't even care if his fucking friends got the
fucking shit beaten out of them. And then Heidi said it almost
looked as if Mark was going to hit Daniel, but Daniel just put his
hands in the air and went downstairs, Mark calling after that he
made him sick. Everyone, Heidi said, was so fucked up they could
hardly see straight, let alone throw a punch. George, she said, just
sort of stood against a wall with his arms folded like he thought they
were all a bunch of assholes and couldn't wait to get away from
them. And Stephen, the whole time Mark and Daniel were at each
other, just sat in the kitchen chair holding a tea towel to his nose,

looking pathetically back and forth between the two of them. "Like a woman," Heidi added with more than a hint of disgust. "He couldn't wait for the boys to head on out and defend his honour."

"So did they find Troy and Jason?"

"Who knows? Probably took two steps out the door and passed out. Where did you get to, anyways?"

"Home."

"By yerself?"

"What — didja figure I took off with Troy Bezanson?"

"Well — no one knew."

Bridget was so much in it.

Margaret P. was getting quite bad. She was getting so bad there was talk about having Albert and Bernadette come down again. There was talk of the hospital, which Margaret P. would not have. She said why couldn't Bernadette take care of her, all she needed was Bernadette, Bernadette was a nurse.

"Bernadette works, Mumma, she has to work in a hospital."

"Don't talk to me of hospitals. My father went into a hospital healthy as the day he was born, one week later he was dead."

"He had the prostate cancer."

"They wouldn't even let me see him."

It seemed like Margaret P. ignored you when you tried to tell her something, but the next day she told everyone she had the prostate cancer. She called Rollie in to her and made him sit down across from her on a chair dragged in from the kitchen. Rollie cried and cried as he always did when Margaret P. told him he soon would die. And she never sugar-coated it with Christian rhetoric the way Bridget would have expected, saying she was about to be carried off on the wings of angels, or that she was going to meet Our Saviour at the gates of paradise. When Bridget was a child, Margaret P. used to go around saying that sort of thing all the time. She was old back then, too, but back then it seemed as if she couldn't wait to die. She walked around with a rosary and Bible, wearing her saint's medals like someone dressed for a journey. Which is what she said she was. She was waiting for Our Lord to whisper in her ear, she said. Peter Joseph Pat always used to tell her to stop with that foolishness and throw him a cigarette. She kept his cigarettes with her, on the other side of the room, on a table beside her holy water and Kleenex. Margaret P. used to tell him that the reason he lived so long was that Our Lord had no interest in peopling heaven with the likes of Peter Joseph Patrick Murphy, or any Murphy for that matter. She would add that last part when she was especially irked. Margaret P. harboured an ancient disdain for the Irish that she couldn't always conceal. She liked to announce every so often that she was "Pure Scotch! Pure MacEachern on one side, pure Colbourne on the other!" These were the sort of proclamations that drove Bridget's father to join an Irish society when he was nineteen, and he still got newsletters from them. In any event, Peter Joseph Pat had died long before Margaret P. did, which maybe proved her wrong about certain things.

But Margaret P. was no longer enamoured with death. She told Rollie straight that soon the life would fly from her body and she would lie rotting in the ground and everyone would have forgotten her by this time next year. But if they weren't careful to bury her on the mainland, the prostate cancer would seep into the ground and everyone would be dead of it by this time next year anyway.

"Goddammit, quit scaring him Mumma! You're making him cry."

"Not goin," said Rollie. "Mumma?"

"Yes, dear, I'll probably be dead by the morning."

"Margaret, stop that sort of talk!"

"NoMummaNoMummaNoMumma no." Rollie spoke like a machine gun, his hands over his ears.

Margaret P. began to cry, too, in a sort of morbid ecstasy. "Yes," she said. "This is what life comes to. This is how Our Lord repays His most faithful servants. He makes us die and rot from our prostates, God bless Him."

Everyone was sort of huddled around Margaret P.'s door. "She never used to talk like this," said Bridget's father. He looked into Bridget's face and said it directly to her, which gave her a chill.

"No," said Bridget, trying to help. All her father could think to do was yell at his mother some more to say a rosary and calm herself.

"Fuck you," said Margaret P. "People like you will go directly to hell for what you've done to me. And burn. The Lord won't have it."

Bridget's father disappeared then in an indiscernible, silent way that was wholly uncharacteristic while Bridget and her mother tried to coax the monster into bed. Margaret P. didn't want to go. Every time they laid hands on her she thought they were dragging her off to be tortured. She was screaming and writhing, and Bridget's mother was telling Bridget to be very careful, because Margaret P.'s bones were so brittle they could snap. Bridget was holding onto Margaret P.'s upper arm when her mother said that and could not stop herself from imagining the entire thing breaking off at the shoulder, sliding out of the old woman's night-gown sleeve. Rollie paced back and forth in the hallway, and Bridget caught glimpses of him when he went past the door, hands over his ears and whispering.

"The neighbours," said Joan, "are going to think we're killing her."

Bridget glanced out the window, expecting to see a face. It was only white. "They'll think it's the wind," said Bridget. "She sounds just like the wind."

It snowed again the way it had on Christmas, and going outside was like being surrounded on all sides by clotheslines with white sheets, it was like being blind. All sorts of wind warnings were in effect, and they were talking about closing down the causeway because the water was coming up over it. They showed pictures on the news, and it looked like a different place. Nobody in Bridget's house knew about how bad it was supposed to get until Robert disappeared to phone Albert. And Albert wanted to come down at once but pointed out the weather reports.

"Take her up to the hospital," Albert said. This was the third phone call of the day, and Bridget could hear every word he said to her father because both brothers had always believed that telephones didn't work unless you yelled into them.

"Balls," said her father.

"Go on, take her up to the Strait Richmond."

"The roads, Albert."

"It's a fifteen-minute drive. Call up a hambulance, if it makes you feel better. Call up Lockey MacLellan's hambulance, Lockey'll get her up there."

"They can't take care of her any better than we can here."

"Horseshit, Robert. Bernadette knows some of the girls that work up there, they're good girls."

"They'll just make things worse."

"My Jesus, boy, it's a modern facility, y'know. It's not like the one on *M*A*S*H*."

Bridget's father straightened up in his undersized kitchen chair. "Well, this isn't even the goddamn issue at the present time. You don't know what it's like down here, boy, the roads are fucked."

"Well, if they're fucked, they're fucked."

"When's it supposed to blow over?"

"Christ knows. I'll find out. We'll be down as soon as there's a break."

"Well, don't you go taking any risks, now!" Bridget's father yelled.

"Don't you worry, boy. Give Father Boyle a call, maybe he can make it over."

"That fat bastard," Robert said, hanging up.

Dr. Bransk lived right across the street, however, and was as a result their family doctor. Bridget always liked him as a child because he had a little toy seal on his desk with a spring attached to its head, and he would let her boing it up and down. And he had a picture in his waiting room of a girl holding a guitar that she had always liked as well. And she remembered he used to give her empty syringes to use as squirt guns. He never pretended to be jolly or overly friendly, the way some doctors did with child patients. The seal with the springy head was the only really whimsical thing in his office, and he seemed to accept it as natural that Bridget would desire to boing it up and down.

His person was familiar to Bridget, as anything having to do with childhood always is, but he was foreign where the town was concerned. The whole time she was growing up, she heard people remark that he was a Polish War Survivor, and she was only now beginning to develop an idea of what that meant. George and Mark used to joke about getting dressed up as Nazis and coming through his window in the middle of the night and giving him a heart attack.

He always came in through the front door and not the back, like every one else, so Joan had no place to put his hat and coat but the banister of the stairs. Bridget regarded him with the surprise she typically felt these days when she came upon an adult she had known as a child. The unease of seeing less hair, more grey, the fact that the adults were always so much smaller. It never failed to be unsettling. Still she saw the dignity of his furry hat with the tight black curls, as if it had been made from a poodle. And his grey woollen coat, rather than a parka with a hood. He looked at Bridget and told her she was big before going in to Margaret P.

"You are not well, Mrs. Murphy?" Surprisingly, Margaret P. recognized him at once and did not refer to him as Beelzebub or accuse him of coming to torture her or anything. The family left him alone with her, as they did when the priest came to give her communion, standing close by in the kitchen just in case. Bridget could hear Margaret P. telling the doctor that she didn't know what was wrong. She sensed darkness on all sides — she actually said that. She was in agony. Her foot felt like it was on fire, but only one foot. She was afraid. Bridget heard the doctor murmuring and peeked in to see that the whole time Margaret P. spoke, he was busy taking her pulse and her blood pressure and listening to her heart.

He sat and had tea with them after, which was something Bridget had not known him to do before.

"I will give you some pills," he said. "I do not have them in my office, so you will have to go to the drug store. Perhaps Bridget will walk up. You are strong? You can stand the cold?" he said to Bridget.

"Sure," Bridget said.

"Good girl."

"What are the pills for?" said Joan.

"They will calm her. They will make her sleep." Bridget was expecting Robert to pipe up at this point that he would be goddamned if he was going to pump his own mother full of drugs, but he didn't. "After the storm," said Dr. Bransk, "I recommend hospitalization."

"And exactly what good will that do?" Robert said, fumbling with a delicate teacup.

"They will make her comfortable," the doctor said simply, drinking his tea like he had drunk it all his life.

"But they won't make her better."

"She is one hundred years old, Robert," said Dr. Bransk, even more simply.

"Then I guess we can make her every goddamn bit as comfortable here."

"This is just my recommendation," said Dr. Bransk, draining his cup with purpose. "You must think of your own comfort as well." He rose then.

People will startle you sometimes, at times when you are entirely unprepared for it and think your capacity for being startled has been irrevocably muted long ago. In small towns, thought Bridget, you are always aware that everybody knows your business and is thinking about you to some extent. When they see you on the street they consult the brief information roster they carry inside their brains. Like: George Matheson. Jeezless punk. Got busted once for possession. Called his mother an old slut. Threw a punch at the principal in grade eleven. That sort of thing. You know they have that information, thought Bridget, but you never know what they think about it. Or if they think about it. And if they think about it, to what extent. Bridget wondered if certain people thought about her a lot. Not just Mark, but people it never even occurred to her would be thinking about her. She could understand people thinking about her and sneering or thinking about her and laughing, but what she couldn't get her mind around was the idea of somebody thinking about her and thinking. Thinking some more about her, beyond what they already had on their roster. Making suppositions and surmises. People you scarcely even knew. The idea was, for some reason, nauseating.

Dr. Bransk set Bridget to thinking about this. He had reached into his bag for his prescription pad just before leaving, and then all of a sudden his hand froze and he looked at them all with an expression of utter vulnerability. Bridget was not prepared for it.

"I have forgotten my prescription pad!" he exclaimed.

"That's all right, Doctor," Joan cooed instinctively.

"I am getting forgetful," he fretted, trying to smile.

"Bridget will walk over with you to get the prescription."

"I am getting old," he said to Bridget as they pushed their way through the white sheets, the disembodied headlights of cars floating towards them from up the street. "I am used to everybody getting old but me. Have you noticed?" Bridget had noticed very much, but said no.

She stood in his office, idly boinging the seal's head up and down as he wrote out the prescription. Now she had to reach down to do it. It was very dark in the office because of the storm, and he had only bothered to turn on the small light on his desk. She didn't know what to say to him now that she was supposed to be an adult.

"And how is your health?" he asked her, eyes down. This was probably the only thing he could think of to say to *her*. Bridget answered by rote that she was pretty good, and for some reason the doctor shook his head. "You will come to me next time, eh?" he said. And then he ripped the prescription out of his pad, very loud.

"What?"

"You did not come to me, I suppose, because of your parents."

"That's right," said Bridget, figuring out what he meant.

"I would have respected your privacy."

"I didn't know," said Bridget.

"It's a shame," he said. "But next time you will know. I should have made it clear."

"How could you do that?"

"The time you thought you had mono, I might have brought it up."

"But I was, like, fourteen or something."

"Yes." He handed her the prescription. "But it would have been a good opportunity. It just never occurred to me."

"Oh, well," said Bridget.

"I don't like to see people suffer," he remarked.

"No."

"But you are fine, now."

"Yes." Bridget was heading toward the door, floating.

"Next time, however," said Dr. Bransk, "you will know to come to me."

No one had ever talked about next time before. Bridget wondered if she should have been indignant or something. She plowed up the street toward the pharmacy, thinking about people thinking about her. People thinking about her in relation to themselves and other things. Using her to support their own theories, to consolidate their outlook. Stephen had told her that Mark would get drunk and then deliver lectures on women. Mark said he knew all about women and what everyone should expect from them. What women would do to you if you weren't careful. Stephen told her that Mark had even tried to lecture Heidi about this.

She hadn't worn mitts or a hat, and her head was being encrusted in ice. When she arrived at the pharmacy, after waiting around a bit, she had just got the prescription filled when all the lights went out. She walked home blind. Sometimes there would be headlights or flashlight beams coming from the inside of houses. Somebody Bridget scarcely knew pulled up beside her and yelled, "Who's that?"

"Bridget Murphy."

"God love you. Can I take you home?"

It was some man, some friend or acquaintance of her father's, who had a plow attached to the front of his truck and was clearing the streets. Bridget couldn't remember his name but saw him in church passing around the collection plate all the time and finding seats for people at midnight mass.

"Why are you plowing the streets?" said Bridget.

"Jesus snow plows won't be out until tomorrow morning. What are folks supposed to do in the meantime?" But it didn't seem to make sense to plow in the middle of a storm.

Bridget remembered that this man was the same man who plowed the snow off Hutt's Pond in the winter every year so that everyone could skate. No one had asked him to, he just did it. Bridget felt okay sitting with him in his truck. He complained steadily about the town, how it did nothing for the people, how the mayor and the council didn't care about anything but protecting their own interests. "Well, to hell with them," he said. "If the people who are supposed to look after the people won't look after the people, the people will look after each other, just like God intended it."

"Yeah," said Bridget.

"I remember when I sat on the council with your dad. Do you know what they used to call us? The dynamic duo, they used to call us. Hah! Hah! Hah! The dynamic duo, just like a couple of superheros. Hah! Hah! Hah!"

"Why did they call you that?"

"Why? Oh, I don't know, I suppose because we were always stirring up the shit. Didn't care for the status quo, you know, the mill was starting up and whatnot and we figured we could make this town great. The school came to your father the one time wanting a football field so they could have a football team, you know, and your dad and I looked at each other and said, Why the hell shouldn't we have a football team? Well, the mayor of course wouldn't hear of it, being a fat-cat of the old school. All he needed was a comfortable chair for his big arse and a fifth of scotch, and he was about set for the evening. Oh, well, I don't know where the money is supposed to come from, he tells us. Meanwhile, he's got this casino project on the go that he just figures is the be all and end all, and you can see for yourself what that came to. So what does your dad do? Whips out his wallet and slams it on the table. Big, fat wallet your dad had, too, with the chain attached. Well, you could have heard a pin drop. I'll tell you where it's coming from, it'll come right out of my own goddamn pocket if that's the way it has to be. I don't know about you, he says, but I think our kids are worth it. Well, you should've seen the mayor. Hah! Hah! Hah! He was looking for his scotch then, I can tell you. Councilman Murphy, I suggest you bring yourself under control at once, he says. He was always saying that sort of thing like there was a flagpole of the purest gold up his arse. I suggest you bring yourself under control before you are *ejected from this meeting*, he tells him. Well, I'm just about to stand up and put in my two cents worth when your old dad leans back, takes himself a good, leisurely look around, and what do you think he comes out with? Why, Mr. Mayor, I don't believe I see anyone here who's *capable* of ejecting me from this meeting. Hah! Hah! Hah! *Cap*able, no less! Hah! So damned if there wasn't a vote."

"And you got the field?"

"Don't you ever go to any of the games there, dear?"

"We don't have a team anymore."

"That's right," the other half of the dynamic duo remembered. "That's right, isn't it. Last one was in eighty-two."

"There's a hockey team, though," said Bridget. Hockey was the only thing any one at school had ever cared about. Troy Bezanson and Jason MacPherson and Archie Shearer and Kenneth MacEachern and Gerard had all played. Bridget used to dress up in his gear at Halloween.

"Don't have to tell *me*," said the man, smiling all over again. "I'm there cheering them on every weekend. Goddamn good team they are."

Bridget told her father that the other half of the dynamic duo was out plowing the roads, and Robert said his name was Hiram Dingwall and he had always been a crazy bastard.

"Hiram. You know Hiram," he kept saying to Bridget.

"No, I don't."

"Sure you do. Was he drunk?"

"I don't know," said Bridget.

"He probably was," said her father. "Ah, Jesus, me and Hiram. Oh, didn't we have some occasions. I could tell you stories, missy, you think you're the only one who's ever raised a little hell around this town, well, Mr. Man. Eh, Ma?" Joan answered Yes in a pointed sort of way that was lost on Bridget.

"On the disability, now," Bridget's father added. "Nothing to do with his time, I suppose. No liver left in him. Figures he can plow the storm away, does he?"

Remembering Hiram Dingwall had cheered her father up for a bit at first. It was gloomy in the house. All the lights were out and her father had his heavy-duty flashlight sitting in the middle of the kitchen table, its glare pointed at the wall.

"You should call him," said Joan. "He could clear the way to the hospital."

"He'd clear the way right down the docks and into the strait if I know Hiram."

Candles had been lit for Margaret P. to keep her from being frightened, but they did no good. Rollie sat in the kitchen chair beside her bed, rocking and blowing his nose more diligently than usual. Every time he got up to walk in circles, Margaret P. would ask him where he was going.

"No," Rollie would say.

"Sit down, dear."

"No Mumma no."

"Sit down, dear, before they get you." And this would always make Rollie look around and sit down again. Rollie was uncomfortable because Margaret P.'s head, propped up against a stack of pillows, was lolling back and forth, and every now and again she would squint horrified at the candles and deliver a long, hoarse shriek. When Joan tried to give Margaret P. her pills, Margaret P. slapped at her and called her a fucking bitch until Joan had to come out and sit at the kitchen table. Robert was on the phone with Albert, saying over and over again that he had never heard her talk like this.

"Yer in for a night of it, boy," Bridget heard Albert holler.

Rollie came in squashing his hands against his ears, weepy. "Raw-hurt he wants to go to the bah-room Raw-hurt!" Margaret P. was shrieking from the bedroom for him to come back.

"Go on up, then, go on."

"He can't see?"

"Ah, the Jesus." Bridget's father looked at her for a moment, but thought better of it. "I'll have to call you back, boy. Himself is looking for the *tylet*."

Bridget and her mother sat together at the table, listening to the two brothers bump and mutter upstairs. Margaret P. screamed and cried for Rollie. They couldn't even boil water for tea.

CHAPTER 16

"I wonder about miracles," Joan said.

"You do, now."

"What do you think about miracles? Do you believe in miracles?" Bridget's mother had a way of talking about things. It was impossible to know what she was getting at. She pounced on Bridget sometimes with metaphysical questions because she was afraid that Bridget had stopped believing in God. Bridget didn't think she had actually stopped believing in God. It was more like, as she grew, she had an increasing understanding that God cared nothing for people like Bridget. God liked little boys and little girls, the priest had said. No matter what they did.

"You never see them," said Bridget.

"You hear of them. Fatima."

"But you never see them."

"What about a little baby? A little baby is a miracle," said Bridget's mother. She had a strange, stubborn face on her that told Bridget she had been thinking a lot about one thing and was sure about it now, ready to argue her case.

"People have them all the time," said Bridget. "That's what we do. It's nothing."

The wind screamed and Margaret P. hollered: "What have you done to Rooooooo-llllaaaannddddddd?"

"I don't," said Bridget's mother.

Bridget didn't see what Joan was trying to prove. All she knew was that she felt spontaneously guilty, as if someone had turned on a switch.

"I know," she said, "but you know what I mean."

"Just because you see something all around you all the time doesn't mean it's not a miracle," said Joan, poking the table with her finger to emphasize her words.

"What are you saying, Mumma?"

"I'm saying *that*. Your criteria for a miracle can't be something that never happens, can it? Otherwise, you're finished before you begin."

"Finished before you begin."

"Do you see?"

"Yes, yes, it's a good point."

"That's right," said Joan, very satisfied for some reason. She went to the fridge and got them a beer to share because they were only going to get warm.

Bridget was to sleep downstairs on the couch to listen for Margaret P. She began to quiet down at around one in the morning. They had not been able to get the pills into her. Margaret P. kept yelling for a toddy, and Joan didn't want to give it to her because it wouldn't mix with the pills. But once they realized that she would never accept the pills, they gave her two hot toddies and at once she began to doze.

Her parents were exhausted but Bridget was wired. She had really offered to stay down on the couch because she had the one beer with her mother and now she wanted to stay up and drink the rest of them by candlelight. She had transferred them all to the freezer to keep them from getting warm but thought it might be even more effective if she put them out in the snow.

Whenever she closed her eyes she saw Margaret P.'s arm breaking off inside her nightgown. She pictured it like a doll's arm with a round, plastic knob at the end and a hole in the shoulder for the knob to fit into. Margaret P.'s room had been lurid in the candle-light, and it was no wonder she was terrified by the shadows all around her.

She didn't know what time it was when she decided to call Alan Voorland. She was bored to distraction and all she could see in her mind were the flickering saints on Margaret P.'s walls. She had the TV switched on, the volume turned down just in case the power came back on, but this hadn't happened. The electric company probably weren't going to bother fixing anything until the morning, just like all the men who plowed the streets excepting drunken Hiram Dingwall. She thought she would call Alan. She thought it would be okay because it was a weekend and he had his own apart-ment now, a few blocks away from his parents in Guelph.

"Oh, God," he said. "Hi. I'll call you back in ten minutes."

"How *are* you?"

"Good, good. It's stormin out."

"Stahr-min, is it?" he said.

"Ha, ha."

"Well dat's how ya sound, lord t'underin."

"I do not."

"Ah doo nut."

Bridget didn't know what to say because it seemed almost as if Alan was picking on her.

"So how are you, Bridget Murphy?"

"Good, good. Drunk. Bored."

"Flattered."

"Ha, ha."

Alan waited a moment. "Sort of a long dark night of the soul, is it?"

"More like a long dark night a me hole."

Bridget said that hoping to liven up the conversation. To make him laugh like she used to be able to when she told him about her constipation and her weeping breasts. Alan was saying little, however. Letting there be silences, which he usually couldn't stand. "And what are you up to?" Bridget said at last.

"Listen," said Alan. "Don't take this the wrong way, but this isn't the kind of thing you can do."

"Eh?"

"Deanna is here."

"Oh . . ."

"Yeah, and. As you know, she's been having a kind of rough time of it lately."

"Yeah . . ."

"She just doesn't need this kind of thing right now."

"But it's only me. You said you wrote her about me and stuff when you were here . . ."

"I told her I had a friend when I was down east, and it went as far as that."

"But I called you before . . ."

"Bridget, look at it from her point of view. I'm getting a phone call at three in the morning from another woman."

"But it's only me!" said Bridget, laughing at the idea.

"I'm just saying. This is a rough time for Deanna. Right?"

"Right."

"She needs to know she can trust me."

"Just tell her it's just me."

"Yeah, I will, Bridget, but you see what I mean, right? You can't be calling in the middle of the night."

"Sorry."

"Where's that big letter you promised me?" His voice changed, deepening with good will.

"Ach, I can't write."

"Well, start writing, you. I really miss you, you know. I miss our talks. I gotta go now, though."

"Yeah."

"Write me!"

"I will."

"From my strange and wonderful Bridget Murphy," Alan said before hanging up, trying to make her feel special one last time.

The call had lasted no more than five minutes, but at least now she knew that it was three o'clock. Or two o'clock, because it was an hour later in Guelph. Or else four o'clock if it was an hour earlier. She still saw Margaret P.'s walls when she closed her eyes. What she never liked were the eyeballs of Christ and Mary and the saints looking down at her. Especially on the three dimensional plaques and statues. Bridget didn't know where Margaret P. got all this stuff, but it didn't seem right to have fake, bulging eyeballs looking at you. The notion of fake eyeballs seemed like a kind of sacrilege in itself. Bridget had never liked fake eyeballs. When she was fourteen, she took one look around her room at all her dolls and stuffed animals, counted around twenty-five sets of fake eyes looking at her, and shoved the lot of them up into the cubbyhole in the attic. Her parents called that puberty, they thought Bridget had outgrown her toys in one day. She had an urge to call Alan back and tell him about that.

The snow storm hadn't stopped. It screamed like a crazed and dying grandmother. You could see zillions of frozen particles swirling in the light of the street lamp, but outside the spotlight it just looked like sheets. The snow dunes caused objects to lose their usual form. Fire hydrants were small, unexpected bumps rising from beneath the white blanket. The bench in front of the post office constituted a bigger bump. The lights were on at the post office. They had to be the emergency lights. The front part of the post office was always kept open and lit so people could check their boxes any time they liked. Sometimes the kids would go in there to get warm when they drank in the wintertime, hoping the cops wouldn't drive by. It wasn't a very good place to go, being so conspicuous. Bridget could see directly in through her living room window. This was why she could never go there.

Mark was sitting in the middle of the lump in front of the post office when she came back from getting a beer, the fluid white coming up almost to his shoulders, most of his body engulfed. She watched him for quite a while, drinking, like he was something on TV.

When she went to sleep she had a dream about all the snow that had piled up against the window of the front door, all the snow being shaken off by someone banging on it. Bam — snow falling off. Bam — snow falling off. Bam — all the snow flying off.

It was actually Stephen. And there was no snow to be shaken off the door because the wind had swept it all away. There was only a fake drift that had been sprayed there from a can by her mother.

"Howlin at the moon," Stephen said.

"You don't want to come in, do you? My parents."

"You should probably come out." He could hardly stand. He was falling against the railing all the time and his usually combed-back hair stuck out all over the place. His glasses were fogged, pushed down the bridge of his nose so he could see.

"Four in the morning or something," said Bridget. "I'm watching my gramma." The wind tried to yank the door out of Bridget's hand and she grabbed it with the other one. "Shit."

"Come on over to the post office, it's not that bad."

"I *can't*."

"Why?" He was so drunk. It was obvious why. He was giving her that fake earnest look that really drunk people always give you which says, We both know what's right here. Quit pretending.

"This isn't fair," she said. "I shouldn't have to do any of this."

"What about what's fair . . . for him?"

"The same goes for him. I don't want to be a part of it." Stephen didn't understand what she was saying. He didn't ever believe she knew what she was saying. He just shook his head and gestured for her to come. He could hardly speak.

Mark could speak. All he could do was speak. He sat against the wall on the floor of the post office, covered with melting snow, a puddle forming. He was wearing his navy coat with a Who pin and a Sex Pistols pin. He'd cut his hair quite short and was wearing a small dark tuque so he looked like a sailor. A sailor with a Who pin and a Sex Pistols pin. He could hardly open his eyes, but he could talk. Bridget was leaning against the mailboxes. The emergency lighting glared down at them.

"Stupid," she said.

"Me?"

"It."

What he wanted to know was, Didn't she know how hard this all had been on him? Did she know he was a mess? She must have heard. Did she know he had gone into the rehab? (Yes — with the monks.) No, this was another rehab, at the Strait Richmond. (How did it go?) How did it fucking look like it went? Did she have any idea what he'd been going through? She could have at least called. She could have at least called. He'd had to do all the Jesus calling around here. Did she think she was the only one having a hard time? Didn't she think they could have worked something out if they'd just kept in touch? (Work?) That was to say, she didn't have to just cast him away. (Him?) They could have worked something out. Mark could have joined the army (Bridget had the bad grace to snort) to make money. Mark's mother said she would take care of him, and his grandmother. She'd never even considered those options, had she? She'd just sent the little bastard packing, hadn't she? Without even letting him see him. (You were with the monks.) He could have got out for a weekend. (You couldn't — it was part of the program.) Extenuating fucking circumstances! They were monks, they understood these things.

Bridget had always thought he went there on purpose that summer. Because he knew. No one had forced him. But maybe she was wrong.

Stephen was sitting in Mark's old place outside on the bench, his head bobbing against his chest like Margaret P.'s, holding a bottle of Smirnoff's between his legs. He was going to pass out and die, probably.

"It's not fair to involve me with this," said Bridget. "I am not a part of it."

"Not a Jesus part of it."

"I'm not. It's not fair." She felt this more than anything.

If Bridget thought she could live in the same town with him and do whatever she pleased and fuck around with the likes of Dan the big fat fairy Sutherland and Troy fucking Bezanson she was fucking crazy.

Mark could get him back, did she know that? His social worker had said. There were channels he could go through. He had been wronged. He was a wronged father, the social worker said. His rights had been trampled.

And another thing. He could sue her and her whole family for every thing they had. His social worker had told him that as well. He was going to do it. Bridget smiled at the emergency lighting. A fortune in wooden ducks and Religious Statues Done by Retarded Man. She was thinking if she could just stand there and listen for as long as it lasted, then maybe she wouldn't have to do it again. At first it had been agonizing, standing across from him, knowing he wanted all sorts of things. But now it was not so bad because she knew it had to be over sometime.

"Do whatever you want," she said. She felt suddenly benevolent and saint-like. She was allowing herself to be yelled at and abused just to appease the tortured soul across from her. It was for the greater good. He would feel better afterwards. She was above it all. She was like Saint Catherine of the Wheel. She didn't even know who Saint Catherine of the Wheel was, but she had always liked the image of a saint and a wheel.

He began to snuffle and kick his legs back and forth on the wet post office floor. It struck her as a gesture full of torment and made her uncomfortable.

He didn't want to do any of those things, he said. He just wanted everything back.

Stephen was throwing up between his knees, which was probably good for him. The vomit was clear and empty. It made a hole in the snow.

And then doesn't Granddad go and bite the dust, said Mark, so that Bridget turned back to him. Losing everyone, he said. Bridget began tapping her foot. She was trying to feel sorry for him. She was thinking about the things she used to like about him a million years ago. She thought he was funny. He could be very funny. One time he wouldn't answer one of her questions except with a grunt, and when she asked him if that was that a Yes or a No, he'd said that it was sort of a Nes. Which had struck her as hilarious at the time. But she had probably been all fucked up on something.

Hadn't they had some good times, though?

They had.

Didn't that count for anything?

Bridget didn't know.

Mark said he was too fucked up and pulled off his tuque. He was nineteen, she saw, and going bald.

She began to slide to the exit, sensing a denouement, but he spoke again. The conversation was not going the way he had planned. He was mad at her, he stressed. Bridget said that was okay. That was okay! Listen to herself, another social worker, Mark said. He spat into the puddle he'd made. The bottom line was that Mark had a son. And Bridget had taken him away from him. That was the bottom line.

The way Mark had said son suddenly made Bridget want to kill him. It was a surprise. She felt all the beer she had drunk gurgling upwards.

"Eat your own shit," she said. She said that because Margaret P. had been saying it to every body of late, shocking her family terribly. So she felt it was the most powerful thing she could say.

"See a round mouth opening and closing toward your tit and live after that," she said. "Live and live and live after that," she said, doubling over.

"What's with you?"

"Puke," she said, and did. Beer.

When she straightened up, Mark was happy. The lights came on and the emergency lights went out. It sounded like *waaaa . . . chung!* She looked over at her house and saw that there were a couple of lights on downstairs. Margaret P.'s window was around the other side of the house. If there were lights left on in her room, they could wake her up and get her started again.

"I gotta go now."

"Stay."

"No." He wanted to be friends now. It had all been about winning. It had all been about making the woman puke.

"Can you call us a cab?"

"They won't be running."

"You gotta go?"

"Yes!"

"I'll see ya," he called. "I'll probably be seeing ya around."

Stephen reached for her incoherently as she went past.

The old thing was up and at 'em, had risen and shone, maybe even before the lights came on. She was in what Bernadette liked to call rare form. Bridget heard the bellowing before she even got in the door.

Robert stood in the hallway with clenched fists, wondering loudly to the walls where Bridget had gone. He was in his underwear, which was disconcerting. Bridget could only think to tell him she'd gone outside for a while, which was the truth. But it didn't matter because she wasn't even there anymore. There were only the walls and the ceiling and the stairwell and the kitchen table and the light fixtures and the refrigerator and the demons that Margaret P. insisted were flying all about to hear her father. He didn't know what was happening around here and maybe he didn't understand the world, but there were certain ways and certain traditions and certain modes of conduct that it seemed to him the average human being was supposed to act in accordance with. And when the average human being failed to comport his or herself in accordance with these modes, it seemed to him that such a human being had to be a few goddamn aces short of a full house or however the saying went. There had to be a nigger in the goddamn Jesus woodpile somewhere. That was only his opinion, but it seemed to him it was the right one, otherwise the whole world would be running around in the middle of snow storms and letting their grandmothers die all alone and not caring a good goddamn one way or another all the worry and grief they were causing those around them.

This was the chaos. Bridget hadn't turned the TV volume down at all when she had switched it on but turned it all the way up by mistake, and the hum of the test pattern competed with her father and Margaret P. for the attention of the house. Rollie was at the top of the staircase, peeking down at them. Bridget thought he looked like a little kid trying to catch a glimpse of Santa Claus in the middle of the night. She smiled up at him and waved.

Margaret P. was not telling Bridget's mother to eat shit or that she was going to suffer a lingering death in the great fiery pit or anything of the sort, but lay back on her pillow moaning and shrieking in the most terrible way as Joan tried again to get the pills into her. She kept asking Margaret P. if it hurt, and when she wasn't shrieking Margaret P. would say she didn't know, she didn't know what it was. Bridget was just standing there, so Joan asked her to go and turn the television down. She thought it was funny her mother would ask her to turn it down and not off.

Robert was still in the hallway in his underwear, telling Rollie to go to bed.

"Raw-hurt, wha wrong, Raw-hurt?"

"Go to bed."

"Wha wrong, no."

"Go to bed."

"No, Mumma."

"Go to bed."

"Hal-fax. Brih-et say stop it."

"Go to bed."

Robert looked as if he wanted to stand there in his underwear all morning telling Rollie to go to bed.

Joan said she thought this was it because she had never seen Margaret P. this bad before, but Bridget didn't believe it. Margaret P. had always been old, had always had spells, "bad turns" she called them, had lived in this room for Bridget's whole life saying the rosary, spitting into Kleenex. Margaret P. had bad turns and every one thought it was "it." But it was never it. It would never be it. Margaret P. did not die but got worse, that had been Bridget's experience. She used a cane and then she used a walker and farted every time she moved, and then she broke her hip and then she had to be held on either side, and then her father simply installed a toilet in her bedroom as that was the only place she ever had to go anyway, and then they bought her a bedpan. And once she had known Bridget, but then she started thinking Bridget was other people, that everyone was somebody else, and then that everyone was a stranger. And once she had said prayers to the Virgin and the Son and even the Father in her more presumptuous moments, and sung songs about fish and bonnie lassies and the cool snow that covered Glencoe and murdered the house o' MacDonald, and now she sank into her bed twisting the rosary into the flesh of her fingers and making banshee noises, the word "God" interpretable from time to time. If she *did* die, she would of course be pleased — seeing all the cherubs flying about, and being with the old people who were once her friends, and meeting God who would remind her of her father. God would remind everybody of their fathers. And Jesus would remind them of their fathers, too. Margaret P. would take one good look around and know that it had all been worthwhile.

But she would not die, Bridget knew. Because there wasn't any of that.